River Tango

Copyright
perri iezzoni
10/2010

www.kakayhombre.blogspot.com

Cover Design by Sydney Howells

Acknowledgements

Thanks be to God for inspiring me in the creation of this work.

I'd like to thank my mother and father, both of whom sacrificed so much to raise the large family I am so glad to be a part of.

Thanks to Jenny, Hannah and Emma for filing up all the nooks and crannies in my life! Thanks to all my brothers and sisters . Thanks to Kathy Giannone, for showing me there is such a thing as magic.

I want to thank Jenny Levina and Dragan Ranitovic for teaching me how to dance. Thanks to my very special tango partner, Sallie Bo Andrews.

A great deal of thanks goes to Karen Lucey and Penny Rosenberger for helping me clean up all the grammatical errors and a few key interactions between characters. They are the reason this book is coherent and readable.

Finally, I'd like to thank the two river guides who have been such an inspiration to me all my adult life: Larry Skinner and Ted Newton, who, along with my brothers, Mario and Chris, and my father, are the type of rugged individualists who make America great. They are standards by which I measure my life.

Thank you all.

perri iezzoni

FOREWORD

     This book is a work of fiction. All the characters in this book are just figments of my imagination. Any similarities they may have to someone in real life are purely coincidental.

     Some of the places are real, like the Lehigh River and some of the names of its rapids. I could not refer to the Lehigh River by any other name because I love it so much.

     I hope you enjoy reading this book. I also hope you find inspiration and meaning to your own lives by reading about the characters and the elements of nature included in my story.

perri iezzoni

CHAPTER ONE

Captain Jack Stueben opened his eyes in his own bed of his beloved city for the first time in five months. It was late January. The Battle at Tora Bora was behind him as he lay in the comfort of a quilt and several fleece blankets in his apartment twenty stories up in a high-rise building overlooking Central Park. Bunny Van Hooven, his childhood sweetheart, belly-dancer and CEO of her own cosmetics corporation, lay beside him.

It felt good to be back in the Big Apple, he thought, but he still suffered from brutal culture shock. Afghanistan was all rock and cliffs, wool blankets, rifles smelling of cosmoline, voices yelling in Pashtun and Urdu: people bleeding, people dying…people he killed. Now he was back in his loft where the temperature was set at 78 degrees. He shut his eyes and told himself he was getting old, getting soft.

At 48 Jack Stueben was an outstanding physical specimen: six foot two inches tall and rock hard abdominal muscles from a lifetime of mountaineering, situps and yoga. The only signs he showed of aging were the crows feet crowding his ice-blue eyes and the streaks of grey in his short-cropped chestnut hair. The flesh on his cheeks was unnaturally white, hidden beneath a beard since the day the CIA ordered him to Central Asia to fight the Taliban.

He couldn't wait to shave it off when he received his orders to return state-side for R&R. After he boarded the military transport in frigid Chaghcharan where he began tough negotiations on behalf of Stueben Incorporated for the rights to mine lithium and niobium, he went straight to the plane's lavatory and dispersed of his facial fur.

His beard was gone but not the memories of Tora Bora, of the World Trade Center bombing or 'The Agency'.

When New York City was attacked he gladly accepted the mission to the Far East, a mission for which he was more than well-prepared having spent a lifetime climbing mountains in the Himalayas and the Hindu Kush. Fluent in Hindu, Urdu and Pashtun, he was a lethal weapon and fighting for America.

Despite having been an inactive agent with The Firm for nearly twelve years, his anger more than made up for his lack of clandestine activity. The city he loved with all his heart and soul, the place where he played, loved and danced, was under siege and he would do all he could to protect her.

But he had to do it working with the idiots in Washington; the ones who always screwed up everything. They botched the Tora Bora assault, he thought, right when we had Bin Laden trapped. The Oil Boys were running the show and there was not much he could do about it…not much but that didn't mean he would do nothing. The political power lie in D.C. but the might of American business lie in New York City.

The Stueben family had been conducting business from their nest in Manhattan for over four hundred years, since the arrival of Peter Stueben and the first Dutch settlers. To Jack, New York was not an American city, it was the world, it was his world. All that lay beyond its borders were merely places where deals were signed to continue life in a city that never sleeps.

On the cliffs of the south side of a nameless mountain in eastern Afghanistan, Jack waited for three days to escort an elite commando unit up a thousand feet of a smooth vertical rock wall to attack Bin Laden in his lair. The commandos never arrived. They were ordered to leave the capture of the man who masterminded the destruction on 9/11 to the Afghanis. Jack nearly froze to death waiting for soldiers who never came, waiting to hear his cover name, Joe Tango, called over the radio.

Now he was here with his childhood sweetheart, Bunny. She attended the same boarding schools as he did growing up in Manhattan. She was his first climbing partner when he got his driver's license and they could skip school to scale the cliffs in the Shawangunk Mountains west of New Paltz, New York.

Maybe, he thought, he should settle down with her and start a family. They could adopt a couple of African babies like Brad Pitt and Angelina Jolie. She would gladly divorce her husband but they both knew Jack would never settle down. His sister, Klara, produced more than enough heirs to the Stueben fortune; Jack would be content to live and love in the city for the rest of his days without ever getting married.

How long had he been asleep? It was dark outside and he could hear the muffled din of the street. He guessed it was 3 a.m. and rolled onto his side to stare at his companion.

She awoke as if the weight of his gaze was enough to pull her from her dreams. She stared back at him for a moment, smiled and bolted out of bed.

He rolled onto his back and stared once more at a crack in the plaster on the ceiling. One of these days, he told himself, he was going to get that fixed. But then it wouldn't be home, he rationalized as the strong smell of coffee brewing and the sound of Turkish Tango music blew in on a gentle wind from the kitchen.

Bunny popped back into the bedroom, bubbly and bouncing. She wore nothing but a sheer cotton sheet and a couple of see through scarves to cover her melon-sized breasts and her very curvy waist. She held another scarf in front of her face hiding her nose and chin, showing only her animated big blue eyes. Her long brown hair fell about her small shoulders like water falling, splashing when it encountered her milky white skin.

She began dancing to the music with the skill of a well trained seductress. Moving in choreographed movements to the vibrant beat of the song, Bunny hopped about the room, accentuating drumbeats with hip bumps.

She smiled broadly with the innocence of an adolescent on the verge of puberty. Bobbing around the room she would fix her gaze on him as she seduced him with her rhythmic writhing. As she looked at him he could see the lust in her eyes growing.

She laughed loudly when the song ended and leapt on top of him, pulling the covers over them as they descended into a serious session of love-making. When they were done she brought him coffee and kissed him tenderly as he drank it, still not speaking.

He fell asleep after they made love again and woke three hours later to find her staring down at him, adoringly.

"Bunny," he said, regretfully, "I've got to go."

He didn't want to go. He genuinely appreciated being here with her and he knew she felt the same way. It was like a great dance encounter when each person can feel that the other is truly enjoying the union. At times like these even the simplest of movements achieve the ultimate romantic affect.

He felt close to her and didn't want it to end. That is why he had to go. He couldn't fight the urge to tell her he loved her, that he wanted to always be with her and that he'd never take another adventure ever again. He knew that was a promise he could not keep. He knew himself too well. He was a child of wealth, pleasuring himself, indulging in all of Life's mysteries and roller coaster rides as he had been born to do. He could never stop.

He had to leave because he felt compelled to speak those words to her and he knew it would be a lie. He loved her too much to lie to her. To hurt her like that. They had something special and he never wanted to lose it.

She continued to stare at him for a long time before taking a long, deep breath and said, "Andrew Jackson Stueben, you are not going anywhere until I've made sure you are getting the proper amount of rest and recreation." She used the name his mother called him when they were children. Her brown hair framed her eyes perfectly as she leaned forward and narrowed her eyebrows as if to say, "I really mean it this time."

"Well," he said with a tone of concession, "I better take a nice hot shower then."

He got up and went into the bathroom. Turning on the cold water, he pulled the shower curtain shut. He went to the towel closet. Here he kept several base jumping parachutes in case he needed to jump out a window during a fire or in a situation like the one he faced now: held hostage by a woman intent on mothering him to an emotional precipice where he would feel compelled to take the final plunge into marriage.

He grabbed a satchel, opened the large window filled with translucent panes of glass and looked outside to survey the jump zone. He could see the busy 97th Street Traverse during the morning rush hour and one of the tunnels that allowed automobiles to pass beneath the pedestrians as they traversed the park, even on icy cold days in January. His breath formed a small cloud that dissipated quickly as he ducked his head back inside.

In a minute he attached the harness and was on the ledge, the main chute tucked snuggly into the crook of his left arm, the pilot chute clasped in his right hand. Without hesitation he threw himself into the frigid air of winter and began plunging through 400' feet of nothing towards the ground clad only in a harness, baby blue boxers and a white t-shirt.

In 3 seconds he plummeted 294 feet before his main canopy deployed, catching the wintry air in its embrace and slowing his descent to a few feet per second. Near the ground he managed to catch an updraft close to one of the 97th Street Traverse tunnels and landed at a walking pace on a snowy sidewalk next to the busy roadway. Quickly rolling up his chute into a ball, he hailed a cab and disappeared into the hustle and bustle that is New York City.

By 8 a.m. he was at his mid-town office where he walked in barefoot and draped in his base-jumper's silky windsail.

Anya, his secretary, greeted him heartily, her close-cropped dark brown hair standing out in stark contrast to the plain white t-shirt and blue jeans she wore. A lawyer well versed in international trade law, Anya was a lethal weapon in her own rite possessing the two attributes no man should ever be pitted against: beauty and brains. She was his savior and secretary and he paid her law-firm partner's wages for her commitment to his secrecy and his family's fortune.

"Nice to see you're baaaack," she said smiling wryly, a slight hint of her Polish accent peeking through her words. "I'm guessing you'll be needing shoes, a cellphone and some money. I'll get right on it. Any progress on the Chaghchakan lithium mine contract?"

In a monotone voice devoid of any clue he'd been away for the last five months neck deep in land mines, horses and bullets, he replied, "Yes, Anya, all three please. I've got a tango workshop on close embrace on 19th Street at eleven and I don't want to miss it." He walked briskly past her through a large brown door into his office. The door shut with a muffled slam as part of the chute caught in the doorjam.

Inside his sparse office whose walls were spackled but not painted, he opened the door to a small bathroom with a shower and turned on the hot water and let it run.

He laughed when he thought that he wouldn't be skipping out on his bath this time. He was glad to be back in his office with Anya at her desk. She was his connection to the pulse of the city. Through her he could lead his life to his satisfaction and it didn't hurt that she was a damn good tango dancer, too, in case he needed a practice partner in a pinch.

A large oak desk inhabited the center of the room on top of an old oak wood floor looking out of place in this modern office space devoid of decoration. Against the window encompassing the entire front wall was a large couch where he often slept. He liked to be close to the hum of the city that rocked him to sleep like a mother singing a lullaby to an infant. Fifty stories up there was not much noise from the street, only a soft vibration filtering through the abyss between buildings to his nest in the sky.

He took a long hot shower and walked back to his office to find a pair of Converse sneakers, a couple of credit cards with his name rubber banded to a wad of $100 bills and the latest smartphone with a yellow post-it note indicating the phone number of the device. Opening a drawer in his desk he produced a roll of duct tape, tore off two pieces and placed one each of the bottoms of his sneakers to allow him to turn easily on a wood floor.

Picking up the phone he familiarized himself with it, scrolling through the screens and menus before sending a text to Anya in the next room asking her to send flowers and chocolates to Bunny at his apartment. A few seconds later he received a text back indicating it was done. There were many smiley faces in the text. He smiled.

By ten-thirty a.m. he was out the door and back on the street hailing a cab to go to an Argentine Tango workshop downtown.

He caught the tango bug after attending a play on Broadway called 'Forever Tango', in 1990. Afterwards, he went to a 'milonga', a place where tango and only tango, is danced.

As he rode in the cab smelling heavily of incense and alcohol, the sights of the city whizzed by his window as blurs of bodies, buildings and automobiles of every sort. He remembered his first impression of tango culture that night. At first he couldn't figure out how men were inviting ladies to join them on the dance floor. They all seemed to know each other and spontaneously decided to get up and unite as a couple in what seemed like a very passionate embrace.

The room was a small ballroom with two rows of marble pillars in the center of the room. The floor was made of three inch wide oak boards and had a deep, rich golden patina after years of dancers walking and turning upon its hard surface.

He asked a tall blond-haired woman in her fifties to dance. She smiled and met him on the floor. Slinging her left arm around his neck she pressed her forehead to his cheek and waited for him to begin.

"You know nothing," she said plainly. "Sit down." She indicated with her out-stretched hand back to the place where she had been sitting, a row of simple wooden chairs and small coffee tables lined up against a wall.

She called herself La Batata and it was she who first explained the intricacies and idiosyncrasies of tango culture. She was a singer who came that night to perform a song called 'Malena.' She was a novice tango dancer, or tanguera, but she was Argentinian and she was well-versed in the rules and regulations of this cultural export from her homeland. He found it odd that an Argentine at her age would be learning the dance that hailed from her own country.

"Cabaceo," she spoke, looking him directly in the eyes with no other intention other than to communicate and make sure he was listening. "It is how we ask and are asked to dance." She held a small plastic cup filled with red wine in her hands and rolled it around the interior ridge of her right hand from the thumb to her forefinger's tip without spilling a drop.

She continued, with the seriousness of an elementary school teacher educating a young student on the fundamentals of language, "it is difficult for a man to ask a woman to dance, sometimes it is the hardest thing for him to do. His machismo is at stake and a man needs his machismo or else he is nothing in his own eyes. Cabaceo enables a man to ask without risk to his manhood. It is done with the eyes," she put her cup down and pointed to her own two eyes with her two fingers and then to Jack's eyes, "you make contact, eye contact, and, if she likes you or she justs wants to dance then she will walk out onto the floor. If she doesn't like you or doesn't feel like dancing she will simply not make eye contact."

Jack said nothing, listening raptly while watching the couples move around the dance floor. It was like no other dance he had encountered. He had learned ballroom dancing in college, a must for any young man or woman with a pedigree or someone who is socially ambitious, especially military officers. This dance bore no resemblance to anything he had ever encountered. There was no logic to it, no direct connection to any particular rhythm in the music of which there were many and yet, oddly enough, they did not appear to be out of sync with the songs. He could discern no correlation between the alluring, sensuous movements of the women and the cues given by their partners.

He found the women, dressed in revealing skirts and high heels, to be very appealing, sexy, sometimes slutty, but always very seductive. He was transfixed by the movement of their feet on the floor, perpetually in motion, drawing soft imaginary lines and circles, like an artist painting some abstract image on the floor of the ballroom inspired by the complex rhythms of the tango music.

The taxi screeched to a sudden stop to avoid another cabbie who had pulled out in front of them. The driver yelled obscenities in Pashtun which made Jack smile, then laugh.

At his destination, Jack paid the cabbie and headed into the lobby of a non-descript high-rise. A small marquis in the lobby indicated tango was on the eighth floor. He rode up in the elevator and arrived ten minutes after the class had begun. He paid the modest registration fee to an elderly lady sitting on a folding chair in front of a small card table.

As he entered the room a collective sigh swept through the women of the room, relieved to add another man to their choice of partners. Many women knew him and liked him. At six foot two with eyes of blue, wealth and in good physical condition, he was frequently sought after by many of the women. He had a reputation for being polite and a competent leader. He should be. He'd been doing this for eleven years now and had been to Buenos Aires twice to learn from the natives.

A woman had told him once, after dancing with him, her face flushing and her knees wobbly, "

Jack, you're like a fur coat: not every woman can own one but all women want to wear one, a real one, at least once in their lifetime."

The room was a lot like Jack's office, devoid of decoration: a wood floor, walls, some with mirrors, a few benches lining the walls and not much else. Most of the women partnered with a man and one couple consisted of two women.

In the center of the room were the instructors for this class. A tall thin man of Serbian descent named Drago stood next to an extraordinarily attractive woman known as Olivia dressed in a fluorescent pink, skin-tight dress with platinum blond hair. Her skin was very pale like that of someone from Scandinavia.

Jack Stueben walked near to the women without partners and directed his attention to the instructors. Everyone was focused on the subject being discussed: the embrace.

Instruction was not something he needed. He was well acquainted with all aspects of this particular subject as well as most topics on the fundamentals of this dance. What he needed more than anything was to be back in the embrace of the tango community, a place where he could remain anonymous and be well-known at the same time. Argentine tango was all about physical and emotional connection, he thought; it had nothing to do with verbal exchanges. To him it meant physical comfort without the need for verbal commitment.

"What we are looking for in the embrace," Drago began, speaking eloquently with just a hint of a Balkan accent, " is a sensual connection. That means we are connected not only by the physical sense of touch but also by the other senses." He took a short breath and looked around the room at each of the students, staring intently at all of them. When he came to Jack, the gaze of his grayish-blue eyes seemed to linger for an extended moment that Jack instinctively knew was a tool of assessment.

The small hairs on the back of Jack's neck stiffened when he felt the instructor's eyes upon him. Out of place as it was he sensed the beginning of a battle between two men when each sizes up the other before mortal combat. His dismissed this thought, owing it to culture shock, jetlag or maybe even post traumatic stress syndrome.

Drago continued, "When we are in tango embrace we are aware of our partner's smell, the sound of her breathing. If our diaphragms are aligned we are attached to each other's spinal column, to their nervous system. It takes a great deal of concentration to perceive all these things but we must do this in order to properly begin the dance. The most difficult part of tango is to allow ourselves to relax while completely focusing on our collaborator. And yet that is what we must do: join in the embrace and allow yourself to feel and hear every emanation from the person you are connected to. When you can do this, then, and only then, will you be able to move as one. Argentines do this naturally because it is a part of their shared heritage. For us, it is difficult for we must learn how to relax and allow ourselves to connect without any barriers."

Olivia looked to him, nodded her head and turned her eyes on the rest of the class for affirmation of the teacher's message.

Jack turned to the woman next to him, an Amerasian woman. She was tall but not too tall, about five foot six or seven, he guessed. She was quiet and seemed a bit introverted.

He offered his frame to her and let her be the judge of how far she wanted to come in since he suspected she might be timid. He was totally in control. He'd done this a thousand times and was certain she was in for a real treat; he was going to light her up like a Christmas tree, watch her cheeks flush and hear her gasp as her breath quickened unexpectedly at the warmth of his body and his commitment to their temporary union.

Then something happened that Captain Jack Stueben, CIA agent extraordinaire, heart-breaker and life-taker, Manhattan playboy, entrepreneur, lady's man, did not expect. She placed her right hand on his extended left hand, grasping his thumb like the claw of a tiny bird alighting on a branch. Her grip told him he needed to move his arm a fraction of an inch towards her to be complete and he did. Then she reached her left arm over his shoulder and placed her hand on his left shoulder blade.

She was close to him. Her short black hair barely brushed his face. She elevated herself on her toes until her forehead was even with the top of his cheek. When she did this he could sense the tautness of her tendons as she extended her legs to accommodate him causing him to become aroused. He could hear the sounds of her breaths falling gently in his ear. She collapsed herself onto his frame in an act of submission…performed perfectly.

He was overwhelmed. He could feel the outline of her petite breasts against his chest but she was light as a feather as if she was not leaning on him at all. Her hair was clean and fresh, absent of any fragrance other than her own natural scent. He felt her ribcage expand so that she pressed herself further into his embrace. She was completely acquiescent and ready to move at his command. He was lost in her femininity.

The music began to play and he feinted to his left. She responded perfectly. He breathed her in, enjoyed the aroma of her body and moved to the side, transferring their weight to his left side. She followed completely, automatically, without hesitation or resistance, like she was a part of him: wanting nothing only waiting for him to move or not to move.

He could feel a certain warmth within her, like he belonged with her. They had chemistry and their coming together created heat that burned like fire. He was confused, how could he feel such a thing, he thought. With that idea in his mind she shut him down completely and cut off their connection, withdrawing her arm as she lowered herself on her toes until she stood flat-footed like an elevator returning to ground level.

He was devastated. What had he done wrong?

He saw the disappointment in her eyes as she looked to the instructors. Something deep inside told him this was a setup but he didn't listen thinking he was still out of sorts from twelve thousand miles of flight and a culture change.

The woman stepped away from him and looked to her right. A tall figure blocked the sunlight streaming in through the window from the street, it was the Serbian and he was explaining something to Jack but he was unable to comprehend the words being spoken. He could only see the woman getting further away and the heat fading like a cloud covering the sun.

Drago stood before him, his hand outstretched.

"You're restricting her movement," the instructor said as he grabbed Jack's hand. He said more but Jack didn't hear a word.

When the other man's flesh touched his hand he flashed back to Afghanistan. How many men had he killed? This is how most of his victims died, with a touch of the hand. Faces flashed in his mind of young men breathing their last breath with his arms wrapped tightly around their necks. He instantly switched to combat mode but he was sure the enemy knew its prey was aware it was being hunted. He let his arm go limp, the rigidity disappeared from his posture and he allowed the other man to mold his body into the shape needed to embrace the woman properly. A gut-feeling told him the death blow would not come here in front of all these people.

"Good, good," Drago said, smiling broadly, displaying a light-blue sapphire embedded in his upper-left canine tooth.

He forgot all about the Amerasian woman as he focused on pretending not to be focusing on the Serbian instructor. He could feel the eyes of the hunter upon him even as he transformed back into a predator, a hunter of lions.

The class was over and people milled about waiting for two more teachers, Little Carl and Penelope, to enter the room.

CHAPTER TWO

The itinerary listed the curriculum as "La Cruzada: The Cross".

He wondered how remedial this lesson would be since La Cruzada was probably the most basic concept in tango. He knew Little Carl, who was actually quite tall, was one of the most widely respected and knowledgeable instructors in The Big Apple. If anyone was capable of taking biscuits and making a banquet of this simple topic, it would be Little Carl, or, as he liked to call himself, Carlito.

There was another reason for his attendance. In the eleven years of his continuing education in the fine art of tango movement, he had yet to hear Penelope utter a single word. An extremely fair-skinned Brit with red hair, bright red lipstick and a face like a mime's, she was Carlito's constant companion. He often spied Penelope sitting with her partner at a table at milongas; and it appeared to Jack they were conversing but he could never prove it to himself.

Penelope always brought her black cat and tiny white shih-tzu to the workshops and the animals sat in the corner on a light blue blanket, each with a small collar attached to a finely crafted pencil thin chain made of miniature links of titanium worth a small fortune.

Inside the room, some of the more advanced students departed and were replaced in duplicate by more inexperienced enthusiasts. The Amerasian woman had a female partner from the first class, a young Russian woman in her early forties. The secret agent noticed toned muscles and could see her movements were that of a practiced dancer. He thought it strange that two experienced women were taking a beginner's class but he surmised they were like him: people who knew that the key to tango lies in mastering the basics, not fancy choreographed patterns.

Little Carl billed himself as "Carlito" but no one ever addressed him by that name. A Brooklyn native, the giant of a man at first glance did not appear to fit the stereotypical image of a dancer. His sullen face and four o'clock shadow suggested Mafioso more than mambo, but his dedication and wealth of knowledge ensured he would be a studio's first choice to induct new members into the world of tango while constantly illuminating dancers with years of experience.

Carlito began with a simple demonstration leading Penelope to the cross. He then explained in simple terms the history and purpose of this movement in social tango. The students practiced the movement and switched partners at Carlito's inference.

Jack had a difficult time paying attention as all his senses tingled with expectation of an assassin's knife. The Oriental woman was next in line of rotation to Jack when Carlito introduced le doble cruzada: the double cross. The instructors demonstrated the movement once to gasps of astonishment then excused everyone for a ten minute break.

Jack made a break for the restrooms located at the eighth floor stairwell outside the studio. Penelope was right behind him toting her cat and dog on shining chains. As the door closed behind her Drago appeared from the stairway and swung his right fist hard at Jack's jaw. The battle-tested warrior ducked and Penelope took the hit full force on the side of her face, knocking her unconscious.

Jack slammed his shoulder into Drago's midsection and rammed him into the sill of a large open window hoping to break his back.

Penelope fell to the ground and the cat, Muffy, a melanotic twin-less Siamese, seized this opportunity to push Buttons, a sugar-white Shih Tzu and partner on the leash, through the rungs of the stairway railing where it fell to the length of its chain and hung suspended above ninety-seven feet of unobstructed open space.

Drago produced a knife and smiled, his light-blue sapphire catching a glint of sun through the open window making it sparkle. He lunged at the CIA agent who instinctively grabbed the nearest object, Muffy, and thrust it into the Serbian's face.

Buttons was yanked back through the railing as Muffy found himself forced into Drago's mug and began clawing the man's nose and mouth, digging in its hind legs and dredging furiously. The knife dropped from his hand as he stepped back onto the stairwell, lost his footing and toppled out the open window. The chain connecting the cat and dog zipped across the marbled floor as the feline disappeared into the open air. Buttons was pulled across the floor and caught himself on the metal casement. The fluffy white snow-ball of a creature nearly turned inside out as the chain suddenly pulled on its thin, fur-covered neck.

Its front legs taut against the pane, the canine dug into the hard stone wall, trying to get traction to pull itself away from the porthole and the open expanse beyond. It was a hopeless maneuver of claws frantically scratching an impossibly slick surface, but the desperation of the little animal overcame the laws of physics and it pulled itself, and Muffy, back from the precipice.

Muffy's mug and paws pressed hard against the translucent glass of the window pane as Jack regained his footing to reach out and pulled the cat back inside the stairwell minus the Serbian assassin's face. Setting it down upon the hard floor, Buttons quickly ran to it and began licking it profusely with the kind of joy only a dog can exude.

Just then Penelope regained consciousness and Jack quickly grabbed her left arm to support her and help her to her feet.

"My dear girl, "he gasped, feigning incredulity and hoping she didn't remember Drago's fist smacking her face. "A man rushed us on the stairwell and I fear my elbow caught you upside your head. Are you okay? You were out like a light."

Jack regained his composure. Only a few moments ago he had been in a fight for his life with a deadly enemy who disappeared like a rock thrown into the water with barely a ripple on the surface; now he was aiding this enigma of a woman and hoping to fool her into thinking nothing happened.

Wasn't she just like all tangueras, he thought, unique, independent, one-of-a-kind creatures from a broken mold.

Jack suggested to Penelope she might be low on sugar and he inquired as to when she had eaten last, hoping she would respond vocally and he would at last know for certain whether she was a mime or a mute.

She looked at him with her thick dark lashes, brown eyes and nodded in agreement. Her mouth opened slightly as if she was ready to say something when her expression changed and she raised her hand to her mouth, touched her tongue and showed Jack her fingertip, red with blood.

Now he would never know

Penelope's injury resulted in the cancellation of the rest of the class. An officer of the NYPD arrived to question Little Carl about the apparent suicide of Drago as the students were putting on their street shoes and began to disperse.

The Russian woman he noticed earlier came over to him and introduced herself as Lapushka.

"Eet means 'leetle paw' in my language," she said with a heavy eastern European accent. "Vee needs to talk. Not here. Come."

Suspicious but still seeking answers, Jack was obliged to follow her to the elevator. Inside she indicated it still was not safe to talk, pointing to the emergency phone and the ceiling fan, she said, "Boogs."

In the elevator agent Stuebens looked directly at Lapushka. She returned his stare with a gaze that said nothing. She was Caucasian but her slanted eye sockets betrayed a strong Oriental, Mongol, heritage. She was a small thin woman, nearly flat-chested but her tone muscles denoted a woman of strength and agility, not fragility. Her chestnut-brown hair was short but not too short to be tied back in a small pony tail like a samurai warrior might have done.

The two continued their staring match until the lift reached the sixty-eighth floor and the doors opened.

Jack waited for her to depart first, then followed as she quickly walked to a door that led to a stairway leading to the building's rooftop. He couldn't help but admire the woman's sure-footed stealthiness as she climbed the steps out of the high-rise and into the sunlight of midday in downtown Manhattan. He could tell a tango dancer by their walk. It takes years to learn this dance while most others dances can be mastered in a few months. It took him three years just to learn how to hold a woman in the tango embrace. After five years he realized he barely knew the tango walk, or caminar, and had to start learning all over again from the very beginning, but it was worth it; now he walked in balance, it helped him on the dance floor, the cliff face and on the battlefield.

Skyscrapers towered above them like mountain peaks in the Himalayas. His soldiering intellect told him this was a good place for an ambush. He felt exposed and he didn't trust this woman, this stranger, but he needed to know why Drago had tried to kill him and she had something to tell him.

"You are Zhack Stueben, no?" she asked.

A seagull flitted overhead, riding the airways better than the best human pilot could ever do: banking, dropping, hovering, eyeing the two humans on the rooftop for signs of food.

Jack still felt like he was being watched.

"Yes." He answered.

"Deed you 'suicide' Drrahgo?" she asked, fighting hard to not to crack a smile.

He replied, "No."

It was obvious to Jack she was a Russian spy. Her accent said she was Siberian, not Baltic. He stared at her coldly, trying to figure out why she had lured him to the rooftop in the first place.

She continued, " Gooood, eet vas my zhob to….'suicide' heeem." She smiled broadly, "I veel takes zee credit for zat zhob zen. Drrahgo veel not be zee lahst after you," she warned, "heeem I know, others I don't. Een tango zee spies are everyveeeeeere."

With that last word he could tell she sensed something, maybe an attack. She crouched down turning her back to the doorway leading inside. He looked down the stairs and saw no one coming. Her hand was on the rubber coating of the roof. She seemed to be listening for something, yet he still could not see any signs of danger. She scanned the other neighboring buildings with the eyes of a hawk.

If it hadn't been for Lapushka, he would have noticed the red dot on his white shirt too late. The moment he spied it was the same moment the tiny body of the Russian spy slammed into his with a cat-like leap. A fraction of a second later the red brick wall of the building exploded as a bullet impacted it, sending tiny red fragments flying in a cloud. A second shot revealed to them that the unseen gunman had the doorway covered and they skittered around to the side of the parapet housing the doorway to the building's summit.

The air suddenly filled with the sound of whirling helicopter blades as a large commercial helicopter rose above the roof's edge. Men wearing black masks jumped out of the mechanical bird's open hatch. They carried assault rifles.

Jack scaled the parapet wall to an overhang ten feet up. He wedged himself into the thin shadow as best he could and waited for the attackers to turn the corner and find him.

Lapushka, using the abundant roof stacks and air vents for cover, made her way towards the helicopter and two of the gunmen.

A lone gunman turned the corner to kill him but Jack dropped from above before the assailant had a chance to look up and see him. Jack was a master at dealing out death. Using the force of his falling body to disable his stalker, he brought his knee to the ground first, grabbed the masked man with the powerful hands of a K-2 mountaineer and jammed the body onto his extended leg. There was a loud cracking sound before the man's body went totally limp and rolled to the ground.

    He quickly picked up the would-be assassin's rifle and poked his head around the back side of the parapet to confront an enemy he knew would be trying to cut off his escape. He saw a masked man coming towards him, unaware of tiny Lapushka leaping towards him like a mountain lion diving upon its prey, a metal scalpel in her outstretched hand, her eyes gleaming with delight. The scalpel found its mark at the base of the gunman's skull: death was immediate.

    He was impressed with the Russian. If only she had bigger breasts, he thought and smiled inwardly. His eyes surveyed the battlefield. The blades of the chopper whirled above them. He surmised it would be blocking the sniper that fired upon them from another rooftop. He could see Lapushka, now armed with a rifle, moving between ventilation stacks like a dancer, keeping herself hidden from the masked man whose gun barrel could be seen from behind a tube of sheet metal. He was close enough to the helicopter that he could have taken out the pilot but he needed to keep it between him and the unseen gunman.

    He advanced towards the third attacker who moved from behind the obstacle only to see Jack too late. Agent Stueben took him out with a shot to the head.

As soon as Lapushka saw the assassin's head jerk back, she fired a shot into the cockpit of the helicopter which veered into the roof, crashing into the rubber mat and through the surface of the structure. She didn't lower her gun however. Peering into the forest of tall buildings with the eyes of a Mongol archer, she squeezed the trigger without taking a breath.

Moments later Jack saw a dark figure plummet from its hidden perch hundreds of yards away down into the chasm leading to street level. He was impressed. Maybe, he thought, breast size shouldn't be a requirement for a companion.

Lapushka looked at him, saw the wolf in his eyes and uttered a gasp of contempt.

"I must go," she said, glancing towards the helicopter lodged into the rooftop, "there veel be kwvestions."

With those words she slipped through the doorway and disappeared.

CHAPTER THREE

Jack filed a report with his supervisor at the CIA hoping to get some more information on Drago and why he was sent to kill him. He was instructed to lie low for 48 hours but that was something this man absolutely could not do; he was a man of action and would not be killed in his sleep. By 9:30 p.m. he had eaten dinner and was off to the a milonga in midtown Manhattan.

The dance was located at a ballroom owned by a wealthy Manhattan socialite of yesteryear who no longer ventured out into public. No one had seen her for over ten years except through a small window near the ceiling of the ballroom where she would spy on the dancers the way a little girl looks in on dolls in her dollhouse.

The music began at nine but the millionaire playboy arrived late to deliberately avoid rejecting a multitude of women new to the scene.

Dealing with rejection, he thought, was a big part of tango and the reason for cabaceo, the rules for inviting partners to dance. Little Carl once told him social tango evolved as a mechanism for the Argentine population to cope with some pretty severe disparities when it prepared to enter the 20th century. After 1880 there were large migrations of European men who came alone to support their families back home. Argentina at the end of the 19th century, as were most South American countries, was a harsh place to live, wars were common. In such a cruel climate there needed to be a system where society perpetuated itself and thus Argentine Tango was born.

It may not have been called 'tango' in the beginning, when it was just a dance performed by the co-mingling of the general population of slaves, immigrants and native Americans. They gathered in "pirigundines," or dance halls, where hired women contracted to dance with lonely workers. Tango also competed with other dances here, such as the waltz and polka. In the Argentina of the 1800s, if a married man could indiscreetly invite a woman to dance, he would participate more willingly and eventually give up some of his hard-earned cash to the sponsoring establishment and the lady dancer.

"Without cabeceo," Little Carl said, "there would be chaos and the Argentines would have no reprieve from their already desperate situation."

Rejection can drive a man or woman to do dangerous things. Rejection was not something Jack ever encountered but he was aware that it was important to be careful in how he dealt it. He often turned down women seeking to engage him in a dance and it was impossible for some of them not to get hurt.

The room was large, the floor was made of black and white marble tiles and there were two rows of marble columns, three columns in a row. One side of the room held small tables with two stools at each; the wall on the opposite side of the room was lined with banquet chairs and women and a few men were seated on them.

One of Jack's old girlfriends, Linda, greeted him as soon as he paid his fee and entered. She was a mountaineering companion for many years before she grew sick of the free-wheeling playboy and became a lesbian. Her companion, like herself, was an elegant woman with brown hair and long legs; no one would ever suspect the two of not being heterosexual except for the fact that neither now danced with men.

They kissed each other on the cheek, exchanged pleasantries and parted.

Tamara, a skinny and scantily clad woman wearing no bra, and seemingly no panties but closer inspection revealed skin-tone stockings underneath, maneuvered towards him. He spied her out of the corner of his eye but he knew that she knew he had seen her. As she angled in his direction, something about the jiggling of her breasts beneath her scarf-like dress made him change his mind and he reversed his course to intercept her and make eye contact.

While she was still yards away he motioned to the floor with his left hand and walked in her direction. He could tell that she was ecstatic and he found that pleasing. Tamara was not the most practiced tanguera but her body felt nice in his arms and catching sight of her breast up close was always enjoyable.

They embraced.

Jack noticed that she made it a point to allow herself to fall onto him. This threw off his ability to lead her to the rhythms of the music. She did not smell of perfume but already reeked of sweat being an aggressive tanguera and much sought after by many unskilled leaders.

Tamara quivered with delight like a little kid in a candy shop. Jack felt a spasm emanate from her lithe frame as he led a leg-wrap and she slid up into him chest first, her pelvis rolling up his thigh like a tongue licking an ice cream cone. She was so completely off her balance that she severely restricted Jack's efforts to lead her to the rhythm or melody of the music and he soon lost interest in her.

It is customary to complete the whole tanda, or group of songs in the same style, sometimes consisting of three, four or five songs, with the same partner and he politely finished the next two songs before thanking her and walking away.

As he looked for an open chair to sit upon, he wondered if she felt his disappointment with her tango skills. She did seem visibly let down when he ended the engagement and he genuinely was concerned about hurting her too much.

Briefly he tried to imagine how it would be having sex with Tamara but another woman had locked her sights on him and his radar detection system was flashing red in the back of his mind. A sixth sense told him not to look up and he kept his eyes trained on the marble floor as he rose from his seat and turned to his right where mirrors covered the wall on one side of the room.

In the reflection of the mirror he could see Gwendolyn Cooper, a tall African American woman with wavy blond hair making a beeline for him from all the way across the dance floor. She was the wife of a wealthy Democratic politician and she craved acknowledgement of her dance prowess in the form of desired male partners. She was not very good and got most of her dances as a result of her frequent sponsorship of tango events.

To his right, next to where he had just been sitting, a good-looking woman in a bright blue dress felt his gaze upon her and looked up at him. He gestured with his eyes towards the floor and she accepted. She began to rise and he pivoted to his right and came face-to-face with the pol's spouse.

With the acting skills of an Oscar nominee he frowned and motioned towards his new partner. "I'm so sorry," he said, "maybe later?"

Gwendolyn grit her teeth but somehow managed a smile and replied, "You can count on it," and sped off back across the dance floor.

Jack embraced the woman and hastily began the dance. He feigned to the left to test her ability to respond to his command. There was a slight hesitation, almost imperceptible, yet he noticed. She was distracted and focused on something other than his lead.

He could feel her ample bosom resting firmly on his chest, unencumbered by a bra, her nipples firm and protruding. A glance downward and he could see her flush cheeks. She smelled like grapes, he thought, maybe apples. When she took a deep breath she drew him into her lungs, melting around him and into his strong muscular arms.

Now he knew what was distracting her: it was him. He was being 'hunted' once again but this time he liked it.

He walked her around the room to the slow, pulsating tango rhythms, trying to think of the name of the artist to keep his mind off his growing erection. Was it Arrienzo? Canaro?

Effortlessly transcribing the music into melodic movements on the dance floor, he led his amorous partner into calesita, turning her on one foot, and into a leg-wrap. Her slender torso came forward and snuggled his abdominal cavity, conforming her mass to his like soft clay.

In tango, as in all dances, one person leads the movement and the other follows. In tango, unlike other dances, the leader must wait for the follower to complete her move. He is, in essence, following the follower, waiting for her to finish so he can begin anew. Each step is complete and there can be a virtual eternity in between the commencement of a step and its execution.

This woman was full of passion, Jack thought, and he needed to be careful or she would have him fully aroused. He might not be able to control himself after months in the southwest of Asia, seeing few women except those clad in heavy black burkhas. Now he was with an American woman, a stalker of men, a sexual gladiator. He was suffering from culture shock and he could feel the hunger growing inside his groin, deep within him.

He fought the urge to merge, concentrating on a time when he plunged into an icy river to escape Taliban foot soldiers in hot pursuit. He remembered the ice cream headache, the pain, the frigid water encasing his entire body as he swam in the darkness to make his escape.

Flight would not be so easy this time for the steely blue-eyed warrior. Her body slid up against his ever so slightly as she began the leg-wrap movement, her erect nipples brushing against his lower ribs. Her abdomen met his upper right thigh just below the hip and her pelvis arched forward just enough for him to feel the outline of her vagina on his leg. Her left leg, foot clad in dark blue three-inch heels with luminescent white stars, wrapped around his knee and swirled upwards, exposing the length of her limb and the top of her luscious thigh which he caught sight of in his peripheral vision.

To Jack's relief the song ended but he still had two more to go before he could break away without insulting her.

Like the goddess Athena, she perceived the prey had been spooked and withdrew back into her camoflauge: the guise of a woman, high heels, skin-tight blue dress cut low to reveal plenty of cleavage, long lashes blinking unashamedly.

Forcing his thoughts to the attack on the rooftop at noon, the secret agent managed to regain his composure and quell his sexual hunger for one more song.

It seemed to him as if she had eased off, maybe he was imagining things, he told himself. Maybe she was naturally an extremely affectionate female. Maybe she was unable to hide the intensity of her passion while engaged in the deep tango embrace, a connection so spiritually invasive it allows each participant to see things in the other they might not even be aware of themselves. A woman in menopause, suffering from hot flashes might be seeking a sexual encounter, something she would not admit, because of a marriage or a deep sense of propriety, to herself.

The third song began. Jack hoped desperately there would only be three selections in this tanda.

Halfway through the melody he began to relax and allow the repertoire of his movements to flow uncensored, without fear of making himself vulnerable to attack if this woman was indeed a sexual predator.

He led a 'pasada' across his left side and she pivoted gracefully, seizing the moment to execute a 'lapiz': a long sweeping motion of the woman's leg drawing a large curve on the floor with the toe of her heel-clad foot, the slit of her dress allowing her thigh to expose itself.

Jack watched her trace an arc on the marbled floor with pleasure, delighting in the delicate vibrations traveling through her extended limb, into her frame and into his embrace like the rustling of leaves by a gentle breeze. Her toe found its way to his left foot and she proceeded to step across it, performing a 'boleo' with her right leg before stepping forward, transferring her weight and pivoting once more to face his left side. Her demeanor was submissive, feigning obedience, waiting for his next instruction.

As she whirled and brought her left foot to meet his extended right shoe, she looked up at him innocently, her expression vacant, her full lips barely open, covered with bright red gloss. He led her to pass once more in front of him and she was again in control of the moment.

Casting her gaze downward but not bending her neck, she pressed her forehead to his right cheekbone.

Soft curls of brown hair obscured his view as he was forced to scan the crowd with only his left eye. Barely aware of the other dancers moving around him, his right side was projecting into an entire universe that is the sensuality of a woman in lust. She seemed to go on forever with virtual mountain ranges of pleasure. Entire worlds were revealed to him as she brought herself once more into his muscular frame.

She seemed somehow taller, he thought, as he realized she raised herself on the balls of her feet, the tip of her left breast dangling against his bicep. Her left hip pressed itself against him as she slowly began to step over his shoe, her left thigh almost draping itself on his with the flimsiness of a soft fabric. Like a snake slithering around a tree trunk in seemingly endless coils her leg began its upwards trajectory.

He peered into the chestnut-brown scenery, felt her soft locks upon his cheek, in his eye socket. The sound of her drawing a breath, a soft guttural noise emanating from a chasm far, far inside her oral cavity, held him spellbound.

Her torso covered him like a blanket, a forest full of trees draped in bouncing bosoms. He was aware of the bottom of her ribcage pushing into his chest, the side of her waist licking his side like a foot-long tongue unleashed from a dream in another dimension.

Her leg continued to slide upward across his thigh; he was trapped in the eternity of the moment; the passion of the pause stopping the passage of time. There was no sound of music playing, the crowd disappeared from his view; she was all he could see and yet he did not see her, all his senses were focused on his sense of touch. He was lost in her world. There was no past here, no present, no future; only Her, nothing else.

Blood began to engorge his penis as her rising thigh breached new ground and made its way over his pelvic area. The tip of his manhood barely made contact with the roving appendage and for a brief moment he entertained the notion it might slip off and he would somehow be able to break free of this enchantment, but that was not to be. Astonishingly, her flesh seemed to roll beneath his member and soon it was elongated on the top of her lower thigh, just above the knee.

Her dexterous limb continued an upward trajectory, firmly brushing the underside of his penis like the giant tongue he imagined roaming all over his body. It was at this point Captain Jack Stueben ceased to exist and his body was commandeered by an enemy intent on his demise. He was incapable of stopping her.

    The song ended. The shell of the man stood there, a huge tent protruding from the folds of his trousers. Taking him by the hand she led him out of the room and into the dimly lit foyer, to the cloak room beyond. He felt animal fur, soft leather and other fine fabrics sweep his face and upper body as he was ploughed into a rack of coats by his seductress.

    In the darkness he let his arms wrap themselves around her as she had her way with him. When she was done, she playfully licked his cheek with her moist tongue like he was a double scoop of chocolate ice cream melting in the hot sun. Then she kissed him deeply, giggled with the squeal of a little girl and disappeared through the wall of coats.

    Jack's legs buckled beneath him and he let himself slide against the back wall to the floor.

    "You can't get this in Afghanistan," he said in a wistful whisper, and smiled warmly.

    Jack caught a cab and was soon back in his own bed, the temperature set comfortably at 78 degrees, his eyes staring up at the cracked plaster in the ceiling. The sounds New York City hummed outside his open window. He fell asleep, glad to be finally home.

CHAPTER FOUR

The sound of water moving is one of the rhythms of nature God uses to bring us into harmony with him. Even if we could not see him with our eyes or hear him with our ears, we would still feel him.

Our sensation of touch is what connects us to the general cacophony of the universe. This truth is self-evident, though rarely recognized for what it is: our Creator's way of communicating with his creations.

The sound of water's movement is the prayer of the Earth presented to us in a form we cannot avoid. It is a very powerful force. It is faith, constant and unrelenting.

This natural rhythm is one of three forces of Nature comprising the entity we know as 'God'. The other two are wind and sunshine. Hope is born on the wind and the rays of the sun are the love that warms us all.

The greatest wonder of the universe is often the greatest sadness in the lives of many. They fail to realize that God is constantly reaching out to them, asking only that they do…or not do.

It is eight years later in mid-May and the foliage of the oak-hickory forest of the Pocono Plateau is in full bloom, draining every puddle it can find on the forest floor. The ground is almost dry and the river level drops as Spring prepares for Summer. The living exterior of the vine-like membranes of what we know to be trees, transports every bit of moisture from the forest soil upward through vast networks of root systems into a dense woodland canopy of leaves hung from branches striving to find the sunlight.

A gentle breeze blows from the south-southwest through the steep canyon walls of the Lehigh River Gorge. The large, fog-covered stream makes its way off the mountainous plateau into the fertile farmland of the Lehigh Valley of Pennsylvania.

A light rain begins to fall.

Tiny droplets of moisture coalesce in the air and fall from the sky. They gently kiss the land and cover the earth like a warm, fuzzy blanket. In the first hours of rainfall, barely any water penetrates the soil of the vegetative mat on the forest floor. The sun sinks below the horizon as the precipitation continues to collect on the surface of the earth.

After thirty-six hours of light but steady rainfall, the blanket is heavy. There is much activity on the forest floor. Root systems transport raindrops up bark highways to green leaves on the forest's rooftop. There is so much upward movement the weight of the blanket goes unnoticed by many except the farmers and a blond-haired man with hazel eyes named Odie Larson. He is standing on the west bank of the Lehigh River, in a steep ravine, thick with rhododendron and towering evergreens, near a cluster of houses known as Coalport.

Small beads of water collect on his bare face and rimless glasses, soaking into his fleece sweater as he stands amidst the falling droplets. It is cold enough for him to see his breath in the early morning light. The ground is saturated. He is here, at the confluence of the Lehigh River and a small stream known as Buck Run, to drop off his vehicle at the end of a whitewater canoe run on the upper gorge section of the Lehigh River. He will begin at a point nine miles upstream, near the tiny hamlet of Whitestown. The humble Odie, an aging athlete in a world of water and a part-time warrior in a world without water, watches the ebb and flow of the rising river. He stares at the greenery with feelings of acceptance and concession, two key ingredients of humility, the place where all learning begins. Acceptance of what the world has to bring him and concession, that what it brings may sweep him off his feet and carry him downstream to his fate. This mind-set allows the river runner to maneuver using the river's movement to his advantage. The water may carry him towards a collision but he can use his momentum to affect a pivot before hand and avoid catastrophe, like a dancer navigating a crowded dance floor.

The time is at hand, the ground is approaching the point of capitulation: the moment when it is saturated beyond its ability to retain moisture.

Succumbing to the effects of gravity, water begins to move downhill.

The new leaves release with the sigh of a fisherman whose nets hold more than his boat can haul back to shore. The weight of the water on the fabric of the forest cannot be ignored. A deluge is released into the watershed and the Lehigh River begins to rise at a rapid rate.

Odie sees the rain falling from the sky, hears the river flowing to the sea, feels the weight of the water bearing down upon the very ground. He is a river guide, the conduit for others to learn what they have forgotten: how to listen, see and feel the rhythm of nature, the prayer spoken for all to hear so they can make their way down the River of Life.

      Tonight, there will be a full moon behind the clouds, shielding the ground from the heavens. Hellgrammites will be born in the water as they always have been after the first full moon of the foliage's bloom and the river's rise. In a few hours, the river will be pushing the edges of its banks. Fishermen will be forced to stay on the banks or be swept away. Scenic whitewater rafting excursions will double their contingent of river guides, a job Odie performed for ten years before leaving to secure a living for his family, in the so-called Real World.
      To Odie, the river is the Real World. The other world, the one with concrete, machines and guns, to him, is a mere illusion.
      This forty-two year old father of two teenage girls, telecom specialist in the Army Reserves, veteran of three deployments to Iraq and Afghanistan, sees the river as a jewel to be admired. It is an education; it is a virtual metaphor for all things true in his life because it is real and not at all virtual. Life flows like a river. There is turbulence, current, obstructions and all sorts of living things. It is difficult to understand what is truly happening within its banks. The surface may be smooth but the undercurrent can be swift and deadly.
      He understands that the river guides us through life, even though we appear to be just bystanders in the event of its movement to the sea.
      Odie is no longer a working guide and it has been over two years since his last deployment to Iraq. Technically, he is retired from the Army Reserves. He knows he can always be called back;

it is something he assumed would always happen...until he died. To earn a living, he journeyed to the cities to work on large telecommunications networks, often for weeks at a time.

Traveling the river solo in his green, Kevlar canoe, lending a hand to those in need of his skills, he finds the process of running the river therapeutic. As long as he is moving downstream he is sane. As long as he is near 'her' he feels a sense of purpose, like there is something else to do in life besides sit in a desert with a rifle and a radio. Lately, he had been drifting away from 'her', towards something new, something soothing and calming.

Hiding the key to his green van beneath a leaf on the ground, he grabs a door handle to make sure it locked. He moves around to the rear of the vehicle, to the bike rack and releases his mountain bike. Unhitching a rubber strap, he puts the bike on the wet, black coal-dirt of the park's rails-to-trails path and begins pedaling upriver towards the town of Whitestown. The rain slows to a drizzle as the day begins in the river canyon, covering his spectacles until the raindrops run clear and allow him to see where he is going.

Just like the Indians of yore, Odie is learned and skilled in the navigation of this section of the river. The arrival of the Europeans in America may have wiped out the indigenous population of the Lenni-Lenape tribe but their ways lived on, as if the very forces of nature--river, forest, sky--chose its successors to continue the traditions of the original inhabitants.

The native peoples of America possessed extensive knowledge of the intricacies of inland waterways and handed it down to countless generations of ancestors. Sometimes that knowledge would be lost with the untimely death of a mentor bereft of a trained apprentice. When that happened, the community suffered and had to relearn the ways of the river through humiliation and perseverance. If they did not relearn the ways of the river, they would find themselves isolated in the remote wilderness of this land that would become Pennsylvania.

The upper section of the Lehigh River has always been one of the most difficult sections to traverse. Prior to the colonization of America, the riverbed was choked with fallen trees from the Great White Pine Forest where hemlocks and pines stood two hundred feet above their roots. The needs of an Industrial Age society led to the arrival of Josiah White and Erskine Hazard, two early entrepreneurs who cleared the riverbed of obstructions and erected a series of canals, locks and dams, considered the Eighth Wonder of the Modern World. The remains of these structures are now new hazards.

In the present, it seems as if the river is calling out for people and they are coming. They come to learn her ways, ride her waves and take part in a dance known as 'whitewater river running.' With the assistance of seasoned river guides, familiar with its many channels and mazes of passageways, always changing with each increase in water volume, day-tripping tourists can experience the thrill of whitewater rafting.

A thick cover of pine trees and eastern hemlocks blankets the cliff-side on the east bank of the river. They seem to muffle all sounds, even the sounds of the light rain falling. Odie feels as if he is riding into a place that is his home, like a return to the womb. All is quiet except for the sound of birds taking flight upon his arrival into their realm. A kingfisher alights from a branch on a tall red pine above the water, swoops down and cries, " kir-kirr-ke-deeeeeee".

This pine is a landmark for the river guides as they navigate the last, treacherous rapids before the Coalport access area. The place is known as Big Red Pine. The tall red pine growing on a small ridge protruding from the steep hillside, stands like a silent sentinel watching the water slip by as the river makes a change in direction.

As he pedaled his way upstream on the path beside the Lehigh River, Odie kept track of the miles by the calls of birds predominant in each section. At two miles, on a steep bend before Big Red Pine, were the ravens, often betraying their clan with rancorous 'rawhks ' and 'rahhhhhwwks'. They dominated the terrain they patrolled, providing truth to the saying, "ravens rule the roost". At 3.5 miles, it stopped raining completely and he heard the "chick-a-dee-dee-dee" of the black-capped chickadees. At 5 miles, near Mud Run and Gould's Hole, when he heard the "PIE-lee-ay-tid, PILL-ee-ay-tid" call of a swooping pileated woodpecker, he met the strangest bird of all on the Lehigh, Old Johnny Rock.

It was Odie's belief that the tall, lanky man in his early 80's, with a full head of bright, white hair, clad in an azure-blue rain jacket, was involved with an elderly woman in town. He saw him frequently heading towards town in the morning and wandering back to Coalport in the evening. Odie wondered if he hadn't spend the night in town. Occasionally, he spotted Old J.R. mowing the lawn of an elderly woman who had a sewing shop in town.

  Mr. Rock did not use a power mower, he used a well-oiled push mower and Odie surmised there must be more to Johnny's story than all the fishing tips he got from him. Odie liked to think of Old J.R. going to "mow his old lady's lawn," as a goal for his walk and a prelude to sex, if it ever happened at their age. He liked that term and often inserted his name into the phrase, as in, "the next time Odie sees Big Jane, he was going to mow her lawn".

  The sewing lady, whom people in town knew as Mrs. Crackers, had a big lawn and it took the old man all day to cut it. It was clear to Odie that Mr. Rock relished each step of the process. He undertook the task like a religious ceremony. Odie remembered seeing the octagenarian with a slight smile on his aged, cracked lips as he eyed up the next section to be cut. The ripened paramour dragged the mower uphill to begin in just the right spot, stopping to sharpen and oil the blades. Finally, he washed and stored the venerable cutting machine.

  I'm sure he gets plenty of lemonade breaks inside the house, Odie mused, smiling to himself as he pictured the elderly couple ogling each other and engaging in the playful banter of lovers.

  This encounter was no different from the last ten between Odie and the elder angler. Old J.R. fixed the biking figure with an awkward stare, as if he were surprised by enemy troops and assumed a defensive posture. It seemed to Odie that he might be tackled by the World War II veteran. Odie stopped to talk to the old man, doing his best to affect a non-threatening demeanor. He braced himself for a sermon on how to fish the river like a pro.

First, Old J.R. told him, in the rambling voice and style of an eighty-four year old man, who had been on the beaches of Normandy and in mountains of the Korean Peninsula, that there were not as many brook trout of late in Mud Run because of a decline in maple trees along its banks.

" The caddis fly...the caddis fly...feeds off of the pollen of the maple leaf....There hasn't been," he said, his head and his hands shaking, the octogenarian's fly-fishing rod bobbing erratically, "any maple trees for the caddis fly to feed on...and now there's no trout. But when those flies are hatching...you want to wait 'til the end of the hatch...because the little trout will be full, but the big guys have big stomachs, y'know, and they'll be able to eat all the way until the bugs are gone. So...in the evening...after a hatch... you'll catch the big browns because they're coming to the surface to feed, long after the little guys are too full to eat!"

When J.R. began to tell the story about two hikers who gave him a hard time for drinking water that dripped down a rock wall on the side of the trail, a place where he had quenched his thirst nearly all his life and a story Odie heard many times before, he knew it was time to skeedaddle or he'd be there all morning.

"They're building up on the hill now, " Odie said, turning his front tire towards Whitestown and putting his right foot on top of a pedal, ready to push off, "that water might not be so clean now." Standing on his right leg, the pedal gave way beneath his weight and the bike rolled forward. Odie waved and the old man slowly turned and began walking down the path as if the encounter never happened.

Whitestown is not a big town. The Pocono Plateau is not a very hospitable place and never supported a large population of people, even in the days before colonization of the New World. Before the 1800's, when Josiah White and civilization arrived with shovels and saws, the plentiful pine trees made the soil very acidic and not much grew beneath the forest canopy except mushrooms and teaberries. Consequently, the water flowing into the river was highly acidic because it flowed through deep layers of pine needles deposited over hundreds of thousands of years. Not many fish survived beneath the surface except perch, sunfish and eels.

A visitor to this river in the days before Columbus, would have seen a very different riverbed than the one he would see today. The river gorge would have been a very dark place, its tall pines choking out the sunlight and dead trees damming up the waterway. All would have been pine needles, rhododendron and mountain laurel and not much else.

During the last ice age, the Wisconsin Glacier reached down to the southern edge of the Pocono Plateau. When it receded, it left behind a layer of trunk-sized boulders everywhere, from Whitestown to Mt. Pocono, all the way north to the Moosic Mountains, an area of about 20 square miles. A thin layer of dirt covers those rocks, so there are not many farms.

At seven miles, Odie could hear the flute-like song of a white-throated sparrow and the eerie, stereo creeping-chatter of a crested-veery. It was to the music of these two avian species that Odie fell in love with his ex-wife as they 'wintered-over', like lovebirds too enamored with each other to think about flying south.

After an hour of rhythmic breathing, Odie entered a trance-like state. The song of the white-throated sparrow and the smell of wild strawberries sparked vivid memories of his past. He thought of the war...of a bombed-out village in Afghanistan. He thought of a renegade marine he should have reported to a superior officer. He could see his ex-wife, Jane Heeney, when she was younger...and happier. Memories of his failed marriage flew by on a projection screen, seemingly right in front of him.

"Damn you, Janey Ann!" Odie yelled at the top of his lungs, uncontrollably. " Damn you! Goddamn you, Janey Ann!" he yelled again.

He was close enough to town that he worried someone on the trail, or in the woods, might hear him. The traumatized soldier tried to think of better things, of anything, to get his mind off of the war, but the only image he could conjure was of a man in a hospital bed paralyzed from the waist down. It was his former first officer from his initial deployment to Afghanistan. He remembered the promise he made to that man over two years ago. A sense of resolve and self-determination welled up inside him. Soon he was back in control of his emotions. Before him, he saw the black coal-dirt of the trail, the canyon walls lined with evergreens. When he smelled the odor of pine, he realized he was back on his bike heading towards town.

He crossed over a road leading to Tannery Bridge, home to the ruins of a long-forgotten hide-tanning operation. The sounds of songbirds and the solitude of the Lehigh River Gorge soon gave way to the roaring sound of Entrance Rapids and

Interstate 80. Odie was near town and veered off the trail onto a well-worn path leading up a steep hill through the woods. This route led up to a baseball field and a mini-mart gas station where he could get a hot cup of coffee.

      The bespectacled river runner had a java addiction. He found this strange, especially since he drank tea during all three deployments to Iraq and Afghanistan. Growing up in Pennsylvania's coal region, tea was as ubiquitous as coffee. He thought his preference for the tea leaf was his mother's influence but he reasoned it was also because nearly everyone he knew simply preferred tea. Not the fancy green and herbal teas favored by yogis and Upper Left-side New York City-types but rather a black tea, the more common and the more bland the better.

CHAPTER FIVE

Chicken's Quickie Mart was brightly lit by the sun as it perched on the eastern horizon. The morning dew began to lift from the areas on the hillsides above the canyon. The interstate bridge over the Lehigh River could be seen from the mini-mart. The bridge spanned the entire gorge, rising nearly 300 feet from the water to the bottom of the span. Before the interstate was built in the 1960s, cars had to drive all the way down to the river to cross, then drive all the way back to the top, a distance of five miles taking ten minutes to complete. A vehicle now crossed the river in less than sixty seconds. Since there were exits on either side of the river, most people preferred to hop on the interstate, rather than go through town to get from one side of the river to the other. The bridge, supported by three tall concrete columns, spanned over the top of the town that lie in the valley below. Houses were built down to the flood plain. The bridge could be viewed from nearly every spot in town and appeared to cross a river of fog when viewed at this time in the morning. The sun sat like a yellow ball on the eastern horizon and the huge metropolis of New York City lay waiting for the endless flow of tractor-trailers traveling in her direction.

Sometimes the city released some of her finer inhabitants upon an unsuspecting America. Today, Jose Morales, a second-generation member of the NYPD, his wife Gloria and two teenage stepchildren, Karen, 12 and Sean, 14, were on their way to go whitewater rafting down the Lehigh River. Jose, who liked to be called, "Joe-see" and not "Ho-zay", stopped at the gas station for a cup of coffee and directions.

Getting out of his blue BMW, its front-right quarter panel dented, Jose stretched. There was a cemetery across the road. His stepchildren pointed at the tombstones and chided each other about their final destination on the trip with "Dad".

Letting out the obligatory exclamation, "Fuck!" he announced to Whitestown, the world and everyone in the parking lot of Chicken's Quickie Mart that he was a New Yorker.

The kind folks of this tiny Pennsylvania town have a name for people like Jose. It is 'pear-head'.

Whitestown is a destination spot for a wide variety of people seeking outdoor recreation: skiing, mountain biking, fishing, hunting, rafting, hiking or just a drive in the hills. The locals always ask visitors where they are from. Since Whitestown is situated at the top of the Pocono Plateau, almost everyone arriving here experienced an uphill drive on a road ascending nearly 1500 feet in elevation.

It was only natural for every answer to begin with, "I'm up here from...."

To the native inhabitants, that answer, in whatever accent, be it 'da Bronx' or Brooklyn, Philly or New 'Joyzy', Hooftie or Boobah, always sounded like, "M'uppear from..." It was not long after the interstate was built before the townsfolk began referring to their many indigenous transients as 'muppears' and eventually 'pearheads'.

Just to make sure people knew Jose was not your average, everyday New Yorker, which all average, everyday New Yorkers must do upon first exiting their vehicles past the George Washington Bridge, he let out a stream of seeming profanities, which, unknown to the rest of the world, were not really profanities at all, but merely nouns, adjectives, verbs, adverbs, articles and prepositions, all derived from the word 'fuck'. "Fuck, fuck, fuckity fuck, fuck, fuck," Jose exhaled, as everyone pumping gas, walking in to and out of the store, even Father Joe taking down the yellow rope that kept commuters from parking cars in the church parking lot, glanced in his direction. Seeing his curly black hair, four o'clock shadow and the dented BMW, everyone quickly surmised his origin and proceeded about their tasks.

Odie and Jose arrived at the double glass doors of Chicken's Quickie Mart simultaneously. The ex-whitewater river guide reached for the right door as the New York cop placed his hand on the left. Odie knew who the other was and what he was doing here as soon as he heard all the F-words, half a block away. He could tell the NYPD baseball cap rode atop a real-life police officer by the bulge of his pistol concealed in the small of his back. The F-words said New York City and his accent said, "Da Bronx". Odie pulled on the door handle and held it open for Jose because he knew the one Jose grasped was locked.

Jose walked in, feeling awkward. Odie perceived the other's discomfort and smiled. Tommy Marsh, an ambulance driver for the rescue squad, bounded through the opening before Odie could take a step forward.

Whitewater rafting on the Lehigh River was a tradition among New York City's police and firemen.

Odie remembered when he was a young river guide, eighteen years ago.

River guides on this section of river do not go in the rafts with the customers, they ride in one-man kayaks and herd the rafters down the river in groups of twenty rafts at a time. The trips are run much like a shepherd moving his herd off a hillside, guiding the sheep away from pitfalls and brambles with catcalls and whistles.

The firefighters and police officers had a notorious reputation for being unruly and hostile towards the guides, especially before 9/11. Odie flashed back to one of the many times he was sitting in his kayak in a calm pool below a rapids section, when he could see an 'NYFD' hat out of the corner of his eye, in the water and moving towards him. He let the submarining public servant get almost within reach of his boat, pretending to be unaware, before paddling away, just far enough so the predator was tempted to keep swimming after him. He repeated this until the deviant gave up or realized he was being played and quit.

After 9/11, Odie wrote a letter to the New York Times, relating how mischievous the firefighters and police officers were and how sad he was that so many died that day. The letter was never published but he needed to write it to keep from crying when he thought of one of those hats creeping up behind him in the water.

So it was that the aging athlete, home until his almost certain redeployment to the land once conquered by Alexander the Great, ran into Jose, a New York City police officer vacationing in the

Poconos, at the end of the cupcake aisle near the coffee island at Chicken's Quickie Mart. It would be a long day for both men, each a warrior in his own right, each striving to make the world a better place, each so totally misunderstood by their loved ones. Their paths would cross twice more before 24 hours passed and for each it would seem like a lifetime.

Odie prepared a cup of coffee with an attention to ritual only practiced by the most fastidious tea drinker. A small Styrofoam container was filled with coffee a little more than halfway before adding hot water coming from the red-handled spout on the stainless steel coffee machine. With steaming hot liquid filled nearly to the rim, he carefully transported the container to the staging area where sugar, milk and lids were kept.

Jose poured a stream of sugar into a super large coffee cup. He pumped a small splash of coffee into the cup from one of seven thermoses. Odie watched with horror as Jose hammered his syrupy brown mixture with nearly a cup of milk before capping it and heading to the counter.

Odie opened two sugar packets and drained them into his cup. Opening a third packet, he poured in only three quarters of the contents before discarding it and the paper from all the sugar packets into a hole in the counter. Adding just a few drops of milk, he carefully stirred the liquid until he was sure all the sweetener was thoroughly mixed. Gently tearing a curved section out of the plastic lid, he secured it and went to the cashier where Jose was shocking the young female employee with his creative use of the F-word, throwing in a few 'shits' and 'goddamns' for variety's sake.

Jose could not get directions from the cashier so Odie offered, confirming what he already knew. The off-duty officer was further dismayed by the hospitality offered to him by this complete stranger.

"I guess the fuckin' sign is right, you do got a fuckin' friend in fuckin' Pennsylvania!" Jose said, trying his best to unnerve Odie just a little.

Odie didn't bite.

He replied with a big grin, showcasing his crooked, yellow teeth, each tooth as big as an acorn, "You're gosh-darn right you do!"

Odie threw the correct change on the counter and bounded out the door.

As the door began to close, he said, "See you on the river!"

Odie could hear a few more F-words as he pedaled away, being careful not to spill his coffee, riding with one hand on the handlebars and standing on one of the pedals, his hip projecting outward. He even heard a muffled, "goddamn m'uppear," from somewhere as he rolled out of earshot away from Chicken's Quickie Mart and towards his own house a few blocks away.

Pedaling to his house, he heard his cell phone speak the name of his ex-wife, Jane Heeney, as he had programmed it to do.

"Message from...Janey-Heeney-she-so-meany," the small black rectangular box uttered in a robotic voice muffled by the rush of air going past him as he cruised down a small hill. He pedaled faster to gain momentum to make it up the next incline without too much exertion.

At the top, huffing and puffing, Odie read the message on his cell phone: *Emma enroute, she needs lunch money.*

His youngest daughter was on her way over to his house from his ex's home three miles away.

She was a sophomore in a high school, ten miles north of town. She was on the track team and liked to jog over to her father's house for breakfast. Both his daughters liked to visit him before school. Maybe, he thought, because they missed him, maybe because they needed money, but most definitely because they liked the way he made hash browns and 'dippy eggs', and chocolate chip pancakes shaped like Mickey Mouse.

Odie pushed the pedals of his bike faster so he could get home and get a head start on some hash browns. His friend, Alligator Magee, an amateur inventor he met while on his second deployment and his first tour to Iraq, lived in a town not far away and was always dropping off gadgets at his house. Odie tested his inventions and gave him feedback on how they worked. His favorite was a grater that made the process of cutting up potatoes for hash browns a breeze. He rode up a steep bank from the alley behind his property with just enough momentum to carry himself and his bike over the top. Odie rolled the bike next to a shed in his back yard, leaned it against a red, wooden wall and strode across his lawn to the back door of his house.

Janey Heeney, Odie's ex-wife, divorced him after he returned from his second tour to Iraq, his third military deployment. She stated in the divorce papers as the reason for separation, "He's gone so often I no longer know who he is. When he is home, all he does is drink. I can no longer live with that man."

As a retired staff sergeant in the Army Reserves, Odie made a decent living. His military pay, combat supplement and telecommunications contract work provided for his daughters' cell phones and school clothes. His eldest girl drove a used Jeep Cherokee that was putting a strain on his finances with the insurance premium increase and costly repairs. Next year his youngest would be driving and Odie feared he would not be able to keep up.

Janey offered to help but he knew she didn't make nearly enough to keep the bill collectors at bay with her work as a whitewater river guide, night-shift ambulance driver and snow-maker at a nearby ski resort.

That is life in the Pocono Mountains of PA: low paying, dangerous jobs that barely keep the wolves away from the door.

Odie looked upon the general cacophony of his life and was pleased: everything seemed like it was about to fall apart at anytime. He felt bad about the divorce but he felt it was a million times better than it was for people in Afghanistan or Iraq, or even people back in the States, like Captain Jack Stueben, his former 1st Officer in the 75th Rangers Regiment, who lost the use of both his legs after being shredded by an IED, an improvised explosive device, during his second tour in Baghdad.

Odie and Jack Stueben had become fast friends during Odie's first tour in Afghanistan. They were in Iraq at the same time, both on their second tours, when Jack was injured, although Jack was not serving as his first Officer at the time. Captain Stueben's legs were now useless appendages and he spent most of his time looking out a window from his apartment near Central Park.

Captain Jack, as Odie like to call him, was just as much a mystery to the middle-aged river guide, as Odie was to the invalid socialite. Odie could not figure out why a man who had everything would join the army to search for Al Queda in the bleak, sun-scorched corners of the earth. He could understand the initial impulse to join after the World Trade Centers had been destroyed. What confused Odie was why the millionaire's son stayed, even after he found out what a cluster-fuck the whole operation had become. He knew the Captain was equally confused as to his presence in the whole wartime operation, having had many drunken conversations over too many beers while on R&R in Kabul and in the Green Zone.

The officer told him many times that this was not his fight, "New York was attacked," he would say, "not the rest of America".

Jack Stueben lived the life everyone like Odie reads about in tabloid magazines. Flying planes to fantastic parties on remote island getaways, hunting foxes while riding thoroughbred horses, climbing the tallest mountains, paddling canoes down the most remote rivers in the thickest jungles on the planet. Odie loved to hear his stories about the wild places, especially any place the grey-haired officer had been to in a canoe.

Of all the tales he related to Odie, the ones Jack loved to tell the most were about dancing Argentine Tango. Having never married, Jack Stueben satiated his need for female companionship in his busy life by attending the most exotic of all social dances.

In the bars of Kabul and the recreation areas set up for the American military in the Green Zone, Odie always lost interest when the captain talked about dancing. Little did he know then the effect this dance would have upon his life back in the States.

When Odie visited civilian Jack Stueben at James J. Peters VA Hospital in the Bronx and he saw the jet-setting, playboy warrior transformed into an invalid patient in a hospital ward, he was overwhelmed.

He could say nothing other than, "How can I help? I'm so sorry...."

His former first officer lay there, stoic, his chiseled jaw and thick hair would not be of much use to him here where everything was sanitary and bleak. He looked at Odie and said, "I want you to dance tango in my place. I don't know why....how..." his voice cracked and failed him, as tears rolled down his cheeks uncontrollably but he steeled himself, drew a breath and continued, "I don't know how I can make it through this without tango. I think I need to know that somewhere, someone, is enjoying this dance for me. I need you...." and then he looked at Odie as if he wasn't sure he should finish the sentence but decided to go ahead anyway, "I need you to tell me about it. I want to hear what you experience while you're learning the dance. Maybe this will help me transition to...," his voice trailed off and he looked away.

The husband, father of two, river guide and warrior, agreed. He would have promised anything at that moment, so great was the pity in his heart for this man, whom he loved and respected as a friend and as a comrade in arms. That night, with explicit instructions from Captain Jack, he attended his first lesson in Argentine Tango somewhere in lower Manhattan.

The lesson preceded a regularly scheduled weekly milonga. There was a beautiful, bleach-blond Russian woman there who had come unaccompanied. She spoke very little English. When he was required to attempt the first movement with her, she faced him, emotionless, threw her left arm over his right shoulder and pressed her small bosom into his chest; her forehead pressed heavily into his cheek. He almost fainted from the shock of having such a beautiful woman embrace him in such a brazen, unabashed manner. He never cheated on his wife while overseas, but at this moment, it became extremely apparent to him that it was now an option...or at least HE thought it was an option. He felt certain that this woman, this stranger, was making a pass at him in the most overt manner possible, right in front of the rest of the class.

    He stayed as long as he could bear, about fifteen minutes. He was aroused by the full upper-body contact with this middle-aged Russian woman, by the sound of her breathing and the soft touch of her hair upon his face. She worked to maintain close contact with him, in spite of his awkward, fruitless attempts to perform the simple movement being taught.

    He was aroused, like he had never been before, even in his youth. This time it was different. He couldn't explain it and even worse, he couldn't control it. It was not as if he ever could control his erections, however, for the last twenty years they usually occurred with some planning or in the privacy of his own bunk. He was extremely embarrassed. Excusing himself as best he could, he bolted out of the room and headed for home...but his erection did not go away.

    It stayed with him as he drove through the Lincoln Tunnel, up Rt. 3 to Rt. 46 to Interstate 80 and almost all the way to the Pennsylvania border at the Delaware Water Gap. Something had awakened inside him and he was confused. He marveled at how alive he felt and how much enjoyment he derived just from being aroused. It made him feel...young! He felt no urge to seek release. What he was feeling was not merely a desire to have an orgasm; it was something much, much more.

As he got closer to home, he realized there was no way he could tell his wife about this.

The captain had one more request for Odie to fulfill; he was to help Jack locate a man who was a person of interest, quite possibly the man who had planted the IED that cost the military man the use of his legs.

Quickly he unlocked the back door to his house, gathered up six empty beer bottles and put them in the recycle bin on his cluttered back porch where there were many unfinished woodworking projects: chairs, tables and moldings.

His eldest daughter, Hannah, dropped by shortly after his youngest left to catch the bus. She was driving to school and the younger Larson girl was not allowed to ride along. In a few minutes she too was gone and a huge hole settled back into his life.

For a brief moment, he thought wistfully, life was as it should be in a perfect world.

These were the times when Odie wished he were more like his neighbor, always repairing his children's cars or doing maintenance on them, like changing the oil or flushing the radiator. His inclination was towards computers and canoes. He found himself just being thankful his own children were healthy and that he had a good job where he could provide for them, even if it meant being away from home.

Odie cleaned up his kitchen, removed the grater-blades from Alligator McGee's contraption and put them in the dishwasher. Going upstairs, he picked up a throwbag, two hand-carved wooden paddles and his lifejacket. He grabbed a waterproof knapsack where he stowed some dry clothes and his camp stove. He packed fixings for hot tea and cookies in case he needed something warm to drink and a snack while on the river.

As he changed into his river clothes (fleece undergarments, gortex jacket and pants), his phone chimed in with a text message from his ex. It read, *working upper today, may need a ride back to my house, okay?*

His ex-wife sometimes drove a flatbed truck belonging to a whitewater rafting outfitter. It held the rafts and gear for the whitewater excursions. Sometimes she drove it back to her house after the day's outing. She was making sure he would be available to shuttle her back home, just in case her boss asked her to drop the truck off at the rafting center where whitewater rafting customers met before being shuttled to the river. This way she could save on gas in her own vehicle.

He typed back an affirmative response, restraining himself from chiding her about her boyfriend and asking why she didn't get rides from him. He reminded himself that Jane was the mother of his children and she needed to be treated with respect no matter what his impulses were or how much she hurt him by making him move out.

She had been dating a hillbilly truck driver from another town and Odie found himself more than a little jealous but also a little worried for her and the safety of his girls.

With these thoughts in his mind, he grabbed the rest of his river rescue gear and headed down the hill to the Lehigh River. His green Kevlar canoe lie waiting for him, hidden beneath a dense thicket of rhododendron bushes just upstream of Whitestown.

CHAPTER SIX

      The concrete bridge enabling Interstate 80 to cross over the upper canyon of the Lehigh River Gorge, straddles the two hillsides like a giant set of talons of some gargantuan bird of prey. An endless stream of tractor-trailers whiz across the mile-long span, heading to and coming from New York City. They feed the metropolis's mammoth appetite for all sorts of goods, wares and foods produced out here in America, the fruited plain.
      Several hundred feet below the bridge and a few hundred yards downstream, smelling of baby oil and Jergen's hand lotion, on a large flat rock shelf jutting out from the west bank of the river, Jane Heeney stands between two 18" tubes of a 14' rubber raft. It is one of twenty she inflated earlier, lifted off the truck and onto her back to place them in a tightly packed circle on the rock shelf. The area was just big enough to hold all twenty rafts. Her short blond hair pulled neatly into a small ponytail, she provisioned each raft with an empty four-gallon bucket, a twenty-gallon capacity plastic barrel and a large rubber sack while she waited for the customers to arrive in two yellow school buses, accompanied by three other whitewater river guides.
      The buckets would be used as bailers for the rafts as they would inevitably take on water during their voyage from Whitestown to Coalport. The bags would be used to store clothes and food. The rafting patrons dispersed beneath her in groups of four to seven per raft. She leaned on a long paddle

braced on the center tube of a raft, pinioned into her chest so that she stood balanced above the group like a human tripod. She surveyed the new arrivals, bouncing, dressed in a helmet, sunglasses and goretex with a large, neoprene spray-skirt around her waist. She spoke in a quiet, yet clear voice, disseminating the wealth of information these paying customers would need to make it safely down the rapids.

The rafting patrons sat quietly in their rafts. They looked like so many sheep being told by the shepherd how they would head out this day to the pasture: one by one, regrouping when they got too spread out, keeping safe, looking for signals from their guides who would be riding in one-man kayaks amongst the raggedy fleet of commercial-grade rubber rafts.

Each person held a paddle and each group was busy stuffing the 20-gallon plastic barrel while the woman above them talked about their day on the river. In the barrel people could store their food for lunch as this excursion would take the better part of the day to complete. Most tried to pay attention to the trip leader as she ticked off particular points of concern, but they were also driven by an overwhelming need to safeguard their precious food items. Their food was their lifeline in this unfamiliar, ominous backcountry, to the civilization they knew to be safe and secure; back to the places where they lay in warm beds at night, ate food when they liked and went to work or school.

Every person wore a mandatory, bulky, bright-orange lifejacket and most wore a lime-green waterproof goretex tunic, rented to them for the day by the rafting outfitter who hired Jane and her coworkers to escort today's crew down the rollicking waterway.

Jane and the other three kayak guides were part of the river guides' union, a subchapter of the Longshoremen's Union. There were seven rafting outfitters and they all hired river guides from the union responsible for making sure the guides were certified and fit to take tourists through this section and other sections of the Lehigh River Gorge State Park.

Jane Heeney was known to everyone as 'Big Jane', the nickname bestowed upon her early in her river guiding career at the ripe old age of 16. The name 'Jane' was quite common among women working in the whitewater rafting business that particular year. Each Jane took on a nickname to differentiate herself from all the other Janes, such as Janey Z, Janetta, Janey Kong or Janey K. At that time there was a heavyset woman who cooked for one of the rafting outfitters. She was affectionately known as 'Little Jane'. Jane Heeney's future ex-husband, Odie Larson, was the first to apply the grand adjective in conjunction with her quite common first name and it stuck forever.

Not big in stature, Big Jane was big in the minds of her fellow whitewater kayaking sisters and brothers, a true legend of the river. She was credited with saving two customers after near-drownings and coordinated several Flights-for-Life from the deepest burrows of the Lehigh River Gorge: allegedly spewing profanities all the way at the hapless victims, as if she were able to reach into the great void of the dead and intimidate them into returning to the world of the living. This divorced mother of two teenage girls was the pride of every woman who knew her.

She was the very embodiment of independence and fierce determination. A skilled whitewater kayaker she was always the trip leader on these excursions. An E.M.T., she was the most qualified individual to handle emergencies that might occur on the water and in the canyon. It didn't take people long to realize she was a capable leader and to submit themselves to her command during a river trip. In a crisis Jane had a knack for finding the most clear-headed individuals and assigning them to the tasks necessary to evacuate an injured person from the river gorge. Her ability to discern the helpful from the helpless made the rare incident for backwoods rescue go smoothly, or as well as could be expected under the primitive conditions in this remote section of Pennsylvania wilderness.

Big Jane liked working on this section of river. It was exciting and the pay was good for union guides. Living in the mountains one skill is never enough and two will get a person's eyes above the water but not the nose. Janey was breathing in Pennsylvania's northeastern highlands, but just barely.

Now standing straight and bouncing slightly on the raft tubes as if preparing to launch herself into the sky like a rocket, Big Jane began her pre-trip safety briefing. She thrust her paddle high into the air, like Thor the god of thunder raising his hammer to smote the evil Loki.

"Welcome to the Upper Gorge of the Lehigh River, " she said with a booming voice, loud enough to be heard by all, louder than the highway above and the river below. "There is no place I'd rather be, right now, than with you all today, going down this here section of the river." Her tone was welcoming, but not friendly, with a hint of a southern drawl for psychological effects, not because it was authentic. River guides learn early that people more readily trust themselves to a southerner on a whitewater river than they would a Yankee. Her grammar was definitely that of a hillbilly, not for a lack of education, rather to gain the trust of her audience who would be her charges for this day. She needed them to know they were placing their lives in the hands of someone who spent all her time on the river and not in a classroom. She wanted them to believe she was not some summer intern who showed up for a few college credits, that she did this for a living.

Jane had given this speech many times and refined each phrase to impart the proper post-hypnotic suggestion. Guiding was not so much about strength and skill as it was about getting people to believe they could actually steer the raft down the river without a guide in the raft with them. A good whitewater river guide never worked too hard and always used the power of the river to his or her advantage. Using not just the physical energy unleashed by thousands of gallons of moving water as the river made its way downhill to the sea, but also its acoustical properties; the sound of water rushing downstream has the ability to put people in a hypnotic trance, making them susceptible to the power of suggestion.

"This is a paddle, not an oar," Big Jane bellowed with a smile on her face and a gleam in her eye, " 'ores you find on street corners in New York City." This line generated a little bit of laughter and caught the attention of those rafters staring at the river in a trance, lost in the mesmerizing sights and sounds of the river: birds flitting about, chirping, white glimmers of frothy whitewater forming and disappearing like tiny horses on the surface of the waterway. "Pretty easy to use, big end in the water, little end in your hand."

She continued in this fashion, letting loose with a pun then imparting useful information behind it. She told them many things about steering their rafts around rocks and through waves; what to do if they should fall out; how to rescue each other and how to stay together in a group.

The speech was not too long, not more than twelve minutes in length and soon the rag-tag fleet of city dwellers were picking up their boats and injecting them into the current.

Big Jane and the mysterious sweep guide, an extremely dark-skinned young man from Indonesia, who wore his long, shiny black hair in a tightly braided ponytail and preferred to be addressed as Mr. Black, set about helping the customers get their boats into the water.

Mr. Black was not his real name, it was a persona he pursued with a passion. Everything about him was black: his lifejacket, his neoprene wetsuit and sprayskirt that matched his black, Kevlar/graphite kayak, paddle and helmet.

Two other river guides were already in their kayaks, waiting to escort the coterie of rafts down through the labyrinth of the first set of rapids known as Entrance Rapids, one of the highest rated sections of the river for turbulence and difficulty in navigation.

River guides on the Lehigh River accompany raft trips down through the Lehigh Gorge. A kayak guide runs through the rapids just ahead of the first raft to show the best route through the obstructions, usually found in the biggest waves. Periodically, the lead guide will ask the rafters to paddle over to the shore on a calm section of water to wait for the rest of the group to complete a particularly difficult stretch of whitewater.

Sometimes, while the people wait, paddles, lunch buckets and bailers will come floating down the river, indicating one or more collisions occurring upstream.

The lead guide's name was Eric but everyone called him 'Haffie', short for half nelson. Several river guides worked with close friends and were inseparable. Eric and the forward guide, Roger, were two such friends. Eric and Roger wrestled often on over-turned rafts at lunchtime and each was known for his particular escape hold. The short and stocky Eric, with bright, red hair and a face full of freckles, preferred to use a hold known as a 'half-nelson', hence the nickname. Roger, a tall, lanky fellow with long, blond hair usually tied back in a ponytail, was known as 'Fullie', for using the 'full-nelson' hold to subdue his adversaries.

Eric was the most skilled wrestler and usually won most competitions. When he felt he was losing, he would use a cheating maneuver, such as a 'nutcracker' or a 'tit twister', to shake loose his opponent.

Like most river guides, Eric was not a model citizen. Taking guests down whitewater rivers was the most beneficial role he could play in society. When he wasn't guiding, Eric could be found selling time-sharing units or hawking honey and 'Vitamin Bee' to local establishments to be sold to tourists as a wonder drug to cure all that ails a person.

Roger was a union carpenter who split his time between guiding and building houses. He was the most skilled kayaker in this group of guides and his role as the forward guide required him to sit near obstacles where rafts were likely to jam.

Both men were in their early twenties and relatively new to the art of river guiding.

Each rapids section at each water level has a variety of obstacles to be considered when maneuvering a craft through it. A rock may be a significant problem for pinning rafts when the volume of water is flowing at 500 cubic feet per second, or cfs, and be a harmless wave at 1200 cfs. Another harmless rock, such as the one known as 'Percolator', turns into a raft-flipping monster wave at levels between 5000 and 6000 cfs. Learning the changing nature of all the obstacles on just one particular section of river takes over a year to learn and only if the student makes time to run the river at each particular level to experience the obstacle first hand.

Types of obstacles vary. Some rocks 'pin' rafts, meaning they are located directly in the middle of the flow and a raft hitting the rock directly will fold around both sides of the stone, becoming a new fixture decorating that particular immovable object. Some rocks overhang the water at lower levels and become dreadful undercuts where rafts are sucked beneath it. Some rocks are jagged and can rip a raft to shreds. Other riverbed formations create horizontal whirlpools, sometimes called holes or hydraulics, that can trap a craft until the river level changes, the boat breaks apart or a rescue line is attached from the shore.

To be kayak guides, students of the art of river running must know where the obstructions are and must be able to maneuver their kayaks through all areas around the encumbrance. To attain this degree of proficiency, kayakers travel to other rivers and navigate rapids of a higher rating than they would encounter on the Lehigh River.

Big Jane and the foreboding Mr. Black assisted rafting patrons dragging their rafts into the river. The novice whitewater enthusiasts succeeded at getting into the bouncy contraptions without injuring themselves or others when they suddenly realized they were now supposed to do something with the paddles in their hands.

A group of Chinese immigrants from Queens operated the first four rafts and made it into the water first but not necessarily in the finest of fashion. Many of them worked at a chain of restaurants and they were being treated to a day of recreation by their employers. One squad of girls from the China Buffet in Brooklyn was a most notably rambunctious crew. The seven ladies, hailing from somewhere near the city of Fuzhou, in the Jiangxi province of China, rarely ceased their high-pitched squealing, laughter and hand slapping as they made it off the rock shelf and into the current. One of the girls took a shine to the dour Mr. Black and it was apparent she was very intent on gaining his attention.

A disgusted Jose and his family made it into the water amidst the group of chattering Chinese immigrants. Jose was not too interested in getting in the water, much to the consternation of his step-children who were so inspired by Big Jane's speech that they felt compelled to show her how well they could manage their boat into the water and down the river.

Two rafts contained petrified Mennonites from Hershey, Pennsylvania, who had the misfortune to be within ear-shot of Jose as he instructed his children to "put the fucking food in the fucking bucket and fucking make sure it's sealed up so we don't eat fucking soup for fucking sandwiches at lunchtime."

Several rafts of middle-aged Indian immigrants from northern New Jersey were there. They spoke among themselves in a mixture of English and Hindu languages. Seemingly oblivious to their natural surroundings, they carried on a continuous conversation. They moved because they were caught in the flood of rafts heading to the river and could not resist the force of the whole group.

Big Jane looked at the Hindis with contempt. She despised most immigrants, a casualty of over-exposure to so many different ethnic groups escaping the metropolitan areas of the northeastern United States for the great outdoors, most within a four-hour drive of the Lehigh River. She disliked the Indians most of all because they usually generated the bulk of her workload.

All her psychological tricks and all her pre-emptive preparations failed when it came to any large group of non-English speaking peoples. It was as if she ran everything on electricity and the immigrants were non-conductive. These kinds of guests required an immense expenditure of communication skills and actual physical energy, making her extremely tired at the end of the day.

Mr. Black, the offspring of an Indonesian father and a South African mother, was extremely helpful with the Hindis and other Orientals. This was the reason Big Jane requested him when she could. World cultures were not her strong point. She was not exactly sure where Mr. Black hailed from but she surely appreciated his knack for handling the English-challenged peoples who seemed to spew forth from the Big Apple like fumes from a smoke-stack.

Equal to Big Jane's annoyance at the immigrants was Mr. Black's contempt for African-Americans. Today there were two rafts of African-Americans from Philadelphia. A group of young lawyers on a social outing, two couples in each raft. They tried desperately to engage the Indonesian kayaker in conversation as he tried to work. Mr. Black lived most of his life amongst dark-skinned peoples and spoke English with an air of aristocracy and a thick, British accent. He had a certain charisma that created a child-like attraction to him by African-Americans. They loved him instantly and gravitated towards him like metal to a magnet.

Much to his relief Big Jane ordered him into his kayak as she helped the last of her group into the water before getting in her own boat. Eric and Roger were with the lead rafts and already a half-mile downstream, passing under a huge railroad trestle straddling the river like a hulking, wooden titan.

The flotilla of rubber rafts began disappearing into the chasm of the Lehigh River Gorge like so many soap bubbles heading for the drain in a giant bathtub.

Jane Heeney assessed the paddling abilities of each crew as she paddled by them in her swift, carbon-fiber kayak. Its sleek design was enhanced by effervescent sprinkles sprayed onto its surface during its manufacture. She tried her best to ignore the Hindi group who were completely oblivious to her presence as well as the coming rapids. They were fully engaged in an intense debate to determine the most intelligent species on the planet. Their voices broke with hoarse chatter and clicking sounds as they conversed in several different Hindu dialects and the English language.

Three of the Chinese restaurant workers' rafts moved steadily into the canyon. The raft full of squealing young women seemed to defy gravity and move upstream in a beeline for the melanomic Mr. Black. In all actuality, their boat was not headed upstream but merely projecting an optical illusion as they were stuck on a small rock and were not in motion. The entire group's simultaneous movement downstream made it appear as if the young women were going in the opposite direction.

One of the young girls, named Vicki Lee, threw herself into the river and shouted in Chinese, "Mr. Riverman, save me! Ha-hah, ha-hah."

Mr. Black parked his kayak quickly and neatly in the calm water of an eddy behind a boulder in the middle of the stream. He called back in a firm tone of perfect Mandarin Chinese, "I don't save ugly turtles, hold your breath."

All the women in the raft ceased their rambunctious behavior and stared at each other in disbelief for a solid three seconds. Suddenly they realized their friend was being carried downstream, away from the raft. As if on cue they burst into action, instantly freeing themselves from the small rock and pursuing their drifting comrade.

Mr. Black knew how to nip this type of behavior in the bud before it became an all day event ending with someone getting hurt. The girl was not in much danger now; if she tried this stunt a little further downstream in the heart of Entrance Rapids there might be trouble.

Good whitewater river guides are experts in rapid behavior modification. An experienced guide knows how and when to allow the river to apply a healthy dose of negative reinforcement. This concept was being applied right now as the strong, deep water, cart-wheeled and somersaulted Vicki Lee before her friends could reach her and pull her back into the raft. The poor girl nearly had her shoulder dislocated as her friends pulled on her arm like seagulls trying to open a clamshell, getting her halfway in and then letting her drop back into the river repeatedly.

Several hundred yards downstream, Roger and Jane were dealing with a cluster of rafts jumbled near a pile of submerged boulders. One of the Hindi rafts was pinned on a rock in a constricted channel. Jane could barely contain her anger as the river quickly pulled the large rubber raft beneath the surface. Four of America's finest software engineers scrambled up onto the top of a rock barely big enough to hold one of them.

In seconds, the water became a mass of floating bodies, buckets, bags and paddles. The air filled with the babble of confused people clamoring for safety as several rafts tried, unsuccessfully, to avoid the pinned raft and were compressed or took on huge amounts of water, displacing its occupants. The sound of Jane's voice could be heard above the prattle, instructing people in the water to keep their feet up near the surface so they wouldn't be caught on the river bottom.

Roger had committed a cardinal sin in Big Jane's Big Book of River Guiding: never sit behind an obstacle you want rafts to avoid.

Big Jane, like most seasoned river guides, knew customers tended to go wherever kayakers sat. Experience told them tourists had no idea what was happening in the chaos of a rapid, yet somehow possessed a natural ability to propel their boat towards the river guide.

If the kayaker sat behind an obstacle and shouted, "Don't come here!" the novice rafters would paddle towards him or her. They would not know what the guide was saying until they were almost on top of the obstacle and it was too late.

It was Big Jane's preference for guides to sit near places they wanted rafts to go and not in places they wanted rafts to avoid.

Jane mentioned this to Roger in her own unique way while she rescued rafters and directed members of stuck rafts on how to free themselves from the raft-jam. She called him a 'fucker' of all sorts of things, pigs and various other farm animals, before turning her attention to her guests.

Roger and Jane operated as rove guides on this trip. Roger was the forward roving guide and it was his job to stay with the leading half of the group. He was to guide them away from hazards. Jane operated as the rear roving guide. She stayed with the back half of the trip until she could see the sweep guide, Mr. Black, whose job it was to make sure no one was left behind.

Jane looked upstream and could see the young Chinese girls as they finally reeled in their whimsical companion. She saw Mr. Black bobbing among the waves like a cormorant, followed closely by the two rafts of young lawyers. She made eye contact with Mr. Black to assure herself he was aware of the situation. Then she dispatched Roger, who was feeling lower than a hellgrammite beneath a rock in the river, to chase after the customers drifting in the current.

All of the rafts caught in the jam were now through the channel, except for the Hindi raft wrapped around the boulder beneath the four men. They stood on top of it like a bizarre wedding cake decoration in bright orange life vests and florescent green spray jackets. Jane sped off down the river after the rafts, her double-bladed kayak paddle spinning like a windmill as she dodged across several crosscurrents and eddies in pursuit of paddles and people.

Mr. Black swiftly propelled himself ahead of the girls' raft and drifted close to the pinned raft. He grabbed the rope circling the perimeter of the raft. Allowing his kayak to enter the narrow channel, he held on as the river tried to pull him downstream. The force of the river caused his long muscular arms to ripple as it tried to pry his hold from the rope, yet he held tight. The raft with the Asian girls edged into the slot and was deflected by the bottom of Mr. Black's boat. It spun and passed perfectly through the opening.

As the river's strong flow pulled his kayak downstream, Mr. Black held onto the rope like a crocodile's jaws on prey it is dragging beneath the surface. The veins in his massive arms bulged as muscles shimmered in the cascading water, caught between two forces of nature: rock and river. The swift current funneling through the narrow channel tried to rip the kayak from his legs but he held firm, his face devoid of expression, the raft firmly wrapped around the rock.

After a few seconds, an eternity to the men standing on the crowded boulder and the young lawyers approaching the channel, Mr. Black's expression revealed what he knew was happening beneath the water's surface: the raft was slowly coming free. Underneath the water, the current found an opening between the raft and the rock. It pried beneath the latex layer, creating a growing separation between rubber and stone. Mr. Black's arms quivered as the river's flow plowed into the opening, forcing the raft out of the water and into the air as all the water poured into one end of the boat.

Yet the dark leviathan still held the rope firmly, even as the raft stood straight on its end. He skillfully used the tension in the line to rotate and flip the raft over, upside-down into the eddy behind the rock, right on top of him and his kayak. Like a circus acrobat, the river guide popped the raft off him while his strong hands grasped the ropes from both sides of the raft. Pulling on both ropes and releasing quickly, he created a springing motion in the raft, causing it to bounce and stand on its side. As the raft tumbled to an upright position, Mr. Black somersaulted into the raft, upside-down, kayak and all. Grabbing his paddle off the floor of the raft, he used his momentum to vault out like a trapeze artist. He rolled into the water upside-down again just before the Hindi men jumped into the raft, two of them still holding their paddles.

It was an incredible maneuver executed by a man totally in tune with his environment: river, rock and raft. Big Jane saw it all as she watched from downstream, peering between the boulders and the waves with a customer sitting on each end of her sparkling kayak. She smiled with great pride at the feat of her sweep guide. She would confirm his story for him when they would meet, inevitably, in a barroom to tell their tales of the day. She'd say it was a classic river rescue performed in true river guide fashion using the elements to his advantage. She would relate how he used the force of the current to pull the boat off the rock, skillfully guiding it as it twisted around on its nose to avoid the customers on the rock. How it landed safely in the calm water behind the rock and not in the fast moving water. She would tell how he used the weight of the raft and the weight of his kayak as counterbalances to flip the raft over in place, remaining safely in the calm water so the customers could conveniently jump into the boat. Not, however, before he used the trampoline like surface of the air-filled rubber tubes to affect an exit from the raft.

He now lay in the water upside-down, his paddle positioned to execute an Eskimo roll, a maneuver used to spin the kayak around into an upright position.

It was a fantastic event. A truly good deed, and, like all good deeds this one would not go unpunished.

As he was coming to the surface to complete his Eskimo roll, the raft of young lawyers, seeing their 'brother' upside-down, managed to come to his side and then ride completely over the top of his kayak. He toppled back over and underneath the arriving raft, its momentum slamming it into the raft of Hindu men. Both dinghies were caught by the current and pulled downstream with the incredible Mr. Black trapped beneath them.

The lawyers' raft took the lead moving downstream. The hull of the capsized kayak was visible. The river guide's hands felt around the surface to ascertain that there was nothing holding him down.

He had only been underwater for a few seconds when a young woman in the raft yelled, "Save him!" just as the dark man's paddle appeared on the surface once more to affect an Eskimo roll.

The young man sitting next to her reached out his paddle towards the kayaker just in time to disable Mr. Black's attempt to upright the kayak once more.

The river guide's head just managed to break through to the surface. He gasped quickly for air and slipped back beneath the water but not before he shot an angry glance at his would-be rescuers.

Now the Hindi raft had overtaken the kayak. It proceeded to roll over it and another boulder on the river bottom, made apparent by the shape of a kayak outlined on the thin rubber floor of their raft.

Big Jane was busy returning her swimmers back to their rafts and did not see the conclusion of Mr. Black's terrific rescue.

The young lawyers from Philadelphia stared at the raft with the Hindu men and the river guide caught beneath, their facial expressions revealing the shock and confusion they were feeling. They were sure they were witnessing a drowning and suddenly felt sick.

It was at this point in the day that Odie finally caught up to the river trip in his big green canoe and, unlike Big Jane, he saw it all.

CHAPTER SEVEN

    Odie knew what the young river guide must be going through, trapped in the darkness beneath the raft, frantically trying to assess the situation and work himself free. Subconsciously, Odie began counting as soon as he saw the black man disappear underneath the raft commanded by the Hindis. He knew the kayaker was pushing up on the raft so he could slide his boat all the way to the other end. He could see when the young boater hit rocks...twice.
    When he had counted to thirty, Odie thought for sure he would see the telltale signs of a wet-exit, the maneuver kayakers used to bail out of their boats in just such a situation, but it did not happen. He was impressed, most kayakers he knew rarely stayed in their boats past the twenty-second marker. He guided his canoe close to the upstream end of the raft where he could now see the edge of Mr. Black's Kevlar boat.
    Forty-five seconds had passed.
    Kayakers flip over all the time. Usually they are upside-down for only a few seconds before they pop upright via an Eskimo roll. They can also pull the spray skirt off the rim of their kayak to roll forward and slide their legs free to bob to the surface. This is maneuver is known as a wet-exit.
    In the sport of whitewater kayaking, the Eskimo-roll is known as a form of self-rescue. In the 1970s, when whitewater river running became popular shortly after the release of the movie, "Deliverance," a story about four men taking a whitewater canoe trip down the Chattooga River in

the southern Appalachians Mountains, most kayakers, when they flipped over preferred to 'bail' or 'swim' rather than try an Eskimo roll. This was owed to the size and weight of most kayaks back then. As boats became smaller and lighter, thanks in part to the proliferation of Kevlar and molded plastics, more and more kayakers began staying in their boats upon capsizing until the Eskimo roll became commonplace rather than a fantastic stunt.

Kayakers take great pride in their ability to right their craft without resorting to a wet-exit. Some come close to dying, as Odie was sure Mr. Black was getting close to himself. To be underwater in a kayak for a mere fifteen seconds is an eternity. It is also the time when a kayaker begins talking to God. This conversation is usually followed by a boater humbling himself or herself and reaching for the ripcord to begin the process of getting back to the surface. Among young men, 'swimming' was frowned upon and the 'swimmer' could expect serious ridicule from his peers, quite possibly for the rest of his kayaking career.

After forty-five seconds, a person in a capsized kayak can black out. Odie could see the fumblings of a desperate man finished with his conversation with God and pulling his sprayskirt off the cockpit, sliding his legs free and straining his neck towards the surface.

He was right there, careful to maintain an open space between his canoe and the raft. All four Hindu men were still looking downstream for Mr. Black to reappear from somewhere out of turbulent rapids rather than from beneath their raft. The younger boater flailed, apparently unable to find the surface. Odie reached into the water and pulled him out by his lifejacket, the dark-brown skin of his face now tinged strangely blue.

Mr. Black gasped, choked and vomited for a few seconds before being slammed in the face with a huge wave. Odie pushed himself away from the raft, still holding onto the young man with one hand and reaching for his paddle with the other. He kept the boat steady as they rode through a wave train using only his hips to keep the boat from capsizing or taking on any water.

Mr. Black yelled at himself, "FUCK...ME...MATE!" as he continued gasping, choking and vomiting, snot running out his nose in a long green line, the bluish hue disappearing from his skin. The military veteran held on, not saying a word for there was nothing to say. He knew the type of resolve it must take to hang in a kayak upside down beneath a raft in the rapids beyond the point when many others would have ejected. For Mr. Black to give up, Odie thought, was an extremely personal humiliation he would find hard to accept, even though the situation was beyond his ability to control. Some kayakers gave up the sport completely, unable to face their peers, so great was their sense of pride.

The canoeist knew what all good whitewater boaters must learn or they will never be good boaters: a person must humble himself or herself before the river, acknowledge that it is greater than he or she and realize that "there, but for the grace of God, go I."

Mr. Black just received a refresher course in this lesson and there was nothing for Odie to say. What happened and what will happen was between the younger man and the river. They were both glad he was alive and unharmed though the rugged Mr. Black was not too sure of it at this point.

    The elder boater keenly maneuvered his canoe, the partially submerged kayak and the humiliated river guide, into a large eddy on the west bank of the river. One wave train, thirty yards in length, separated them and the calm water where Big Jane and her entourage collected themselves. He made eye contact with Jane. Without a word or a signal from her former spouse, her companion for almost twenty years, she knew something must have happened. The lack of concern in his eyes told her everything was okay and she turned her attention back to the customers in their rafts. Odie waited with Mr. Black in silence, his puking and choking was subsiding. The young man began to regain his composure.

    "Fuck me, mate," he said to himself for the tenth time. His expression was distraught, searching, frantic. He was near tears.

    Odie watched. He had been in the same place a few times. He suspected the diminished man, shoulder-deep in the water, was considering walking off the river. The only way he could go on, Odie thought, was if he chose to learn and relinquish his pride. A person must be humble before the river, not just humble to the river. A person must be humble before the world, before nature, before Life, before God. When faced with one's own mortality, everyone has that conversation with God. That is how he or she knows there is a God. When the River humbles you, when Life humbles you, he mused, watching Mr. Black stare intensely at the water, no longer choking but still blowing snot out of his nose, you must choose to learn from that experience and you must say to yourself, "everything is greater than I."

All the lessons he learned in life began with humbling experiences which taught him to proceed with caution and humility. That is how he made it down the river all these times, and not just this river but many more up and down the east coast. That is how he made it back from the war...three times.

It is moments such as this that make a person's relationship with the River a much more personal and rewarding experience. Odie often wondered about death. Was it the ultimate humbling experience? If so, was it then proof there was life after death? If humiliation was the beginning of all Life's lessons would it be safe to assume that death was just the beginning of another lesson?

Odie made eye contact with Mr. Black and he knew he was done. Either he had chosen to learn or not-to-learn, whatever his decision it was between him and God. He hoped the Indonesian man he liked so much would learn and get back in his kayak. It was floating in the eddy just beneath the surface of the water, not far from the two men.

Mr. Black stood up in the waist deep water and waded over to his submerged vessel. He pushed one end towards shore and grabbed the other end, lifting it out of the river, the cockpit facing down. Water gushed out of his kayak. He slid the boat down upon his knee and tilted it back and forth until he emptied the boat. He slid himself back in, his hand holding onto the canoe for support while Odie kept his kayak stable. He could tell the Indonesian man's arms still quivered uncontrollably from the experience.

The former river guide noticed a large scrape on Mr. Black's right shoulder.

"Hey, Blackman!" he said in a tone that was neither soft nor hard, but firm,"you got a big scrape on your shoulder, you okay?"

Mr. Black looked to his left, then to Odie who shook his head and pointed to the other shoulder.

He looked right, shrugged and said, "No way big fella, I'm alright." With a grunt he pushed himself away from the canoe. Sinking his long arms into the water up to his elbows, he hand-paddled himself downriver to where Big Jane sat waiting with his kayak paddle.

Big Jane gave a nod to Fullie who was doing cartwheels with his kayak while the rafters bailed and hung on to tree limbs to keep from moving downstream.

With a voice as loud as a foghorn, Fullie yelled, "OKAAAAAY, LET'S GOOOO!" and all the rafts released their hold on the shore and moved simultaneously, like a huge flock of birds taking flight. Everybody was chattering and several people were busy splashing and smacking their paddles in the water. Sounds of laughter and cries of glee filled the air.

Big Jane looked to Odie. He sent his canoe in her direction with one skillful, well-placed paddle stroke. His boat caught a fast current and it sped him across the river to a point right next to his ex-wife's black kayak.

"M.B. got totally trashed," Odie said, answering Jane's inquisitive look.

"What happened?" Jane asked, "all I saw was Blackie pulling the raft off the rock and doing one of those kayak/raft flips..." her voice trailed off. She was at a loss for words and worried about her fellow guide.

Odie explained, "He forgot about the black yuppies and they ran him over, then fucked up his roll. Then he got run over again by the boys from Bangalore...Jane," he added, his voice dropping a few decibels as he pulled his boat closer to hers, "his face was blue when he came up and he swallowed a lot of water. Keep an eye on him in case he goes into shock."

Jane nodded in agreement.

Pushing off his canoe with her hand, she turned her attention back to the group. Mr. Black sat sulking in an eddy at the rear of the noisy rubber armada. Haffie and Fullie honed in on a group of young women in several rafts. The young men performed boat tricks, Eskimo rolls and cartwheels, all the while pretending not to notice the young ladies who pretended not to be impressed by their attention.

The six Indian men were all back together in the same raft, oblivious to the fact their guide nearly drowned while trapped beneath their raft in the last set of rapids. Once more they engaged in serious debate, as people are inclined to do when passing through vast expanses of nature. They had solved all of mankind's problems and moved the discussion back to which species was the most intelligent.

" No, no, no, " Raj objected, his voice cracking with his New Delhi accent, piercing the symphony of voices, buckets rattling and paddles splashing while the flotilla drifted along together, everyone paddling lazily and at random. "Viruses cannot be the most intelligent species. They are not wide spread. It is the plants most wide spread: corn, sugar, wheat. These plants use US to spread their seeds, WE are just pawns, caught in a war between sugar and corn and wheat plants!"

Jose's distinct Bronx accent could be heard easily above the din, cursing his stepchildren for their inability to row in unison or on his command. His step-children laughed at him with obvious disregard. He sat in the back of the raft, his legs straddling the outer tube, one foot in the water, reaching his oar far beyond the boat to turn the raft.

Odie drifted along with the crowd, enjoying their company and remembering a time when he too was a guide.

When he passed by Jose he commented on his foot being outside the raft and warned, "the witchey woman will be yelling at you!" Then he laughed and paddled away.

"Hey, I remember that guy," Jose said to his wife, "he was at the quick mart this morning. Remember?"

A pair of mallards came flying upstream, like two fighter jets on a bombing run, their wings beating to a steady, fast rhythm, as they passed over the rafters, forty feet above the water. The birds went mostly unnoticed by all except the river guides and a couple from Bayonne, New Jersey, who were in the only raft containing just two persons.

The woman was of Italian-American descent with light olive-brown skin. Her long black hair was pulled into an intricately braided ponytail. She was in her early fifties and she was here with her ailing husband, a stout man of Greek ancestry with short pepper-grey hair. They were both short in stature. Like the ducks, they passed mostly unnoticed among the group.

The couple had been down this river many times and arranged to have a raft small enough for the two to row easily. The woman called herself Cassie and the man was named Tiresias. He was blind in one eye and wore thick black-rimmed glasses.

Tiresias contracted the AIDS virus seven years earlier and was afflicted with cancer of the kidney and spine. His doctors told him he had six months to live and implanted a morphine-drip next to his spine to help ease the pain.

He and Cassie loved their trips down the river.

They began their sojourns when they discovered he contracted the AIDS virus from a blood transfusion during a medical treatment for blood poisoning. Until then the couple had never taken a trip outside of the New York metropolitan area, content to live in their little Greek neighborhood by the Hudson River.

It was Tiresias' intent to take his own life at lunchtime after concocting a tea of poison hemlock and drinking it.

He devised a plan to achieve a peaceful, painless end to his life. He thought it very traditional and also 100% organic. He was using a local herb to make the suicide look like an accidental poisoning so his wife would be eligible for some insurance money.

His passing would mimick Socrates, the famous philosopher forced to drink poison hemlock at his execution in 399 B.C.E.

They found the weed growing on the side of the Lehigh River and planned to harvest their deadly crop during the first half of their river excursion. They were surprised to find a large concentration of the white flowering plant at the first pull-over in the pool below Entrance Rapids. Tiresias took this as a sign from God that he was doing the right thing and was in good spirits.

Cassie looked forward to lunch with a dread she could not hide from her beloved husband. She supported her husband's desire for relief but did not want to lose him.

CHAPTER EIGHT

Odie passed among the group, getting strange looks because of the size of his canoe and the fact that it was so different from the kayaks the river guides paddled.

There were many rapids in between Entrance Rapids and the designated lunch spot, both named and unnamed. Beneath Tannery Bridge, a half mile before Triple Drop Rapids, Odie pulled into an eddy next to a bridge abutment. He watched Haffie and Fullie play on a unique phenomenon of rivers: the standing wave.

A standing wave is a wave created by an obstruction on the river bottom that produces a consistent, wave-shaped path for the water to travel. The wave may pulsate, growing bigger or shrinking smaller but it does not disappear completely. Unlike a wave at the beach which eventually runs up on the shore and slinks back into the ocean, a standing wave only dissipates when the river's water level drops.

When boaters began traveling down whitewater rivers, they soon discovered one of the greatest, most addictive joys of the water: surfing. Much like its oceanic cousin, surfing a wave on a river involves paddling upstream, just as a canoe or kayak is about to encounter the standing wave. If the paddler is skilled, then he or she can reach a point where the force of gravity cancels out the force of the current and the boat stops moving downstream. In this state of equilibrium the craft is constantly falling down the face of the wave, upstream, while the river's current is constantly pushing the hull downstream. Once equilibrium is achieved a kayaker or canoeist can use their paddle as a rudder to maneuver across the face of the wave, back and forth, until equilibrium is lost and he or she is tossed off the wave like a bull rider at a rodeo.

Odie goaded the two young river guides into accepting the challenge of who could make it onto the wave with the fewest number of strokes. He let Haffie and Fullie try three times each. He then pulled out of the eddy and ferried onto the wave with just one paddle stroke. Angling his canoe to the left, across the wave and then to the right, Odie shot off the wave in his big, green canoe, waved, smiled and headed downstream.

Odie watched the surfing couple play on the wave like youthful river otters, zipping back and forth, popping up out of the water, slamming into each other and intentionally reaching out to tip over one another's kayaks.

Customers in rafts surrounded him as the current carried them downstream, the Nelson brothers fading into specs as the distance between them increased.

They were abandoning their posts and he knew Jane would be angry with them but he was sure they didn't care, they were lost in the moment, such was the allure of wave surfing on kayakers. They were lost in the dance of the river; each different water level was like a new song and every wave was a new dance hall. To be able to share this experience with another of the same ability was like engaging in a dangerous ménage a trios: if performed with respect and deference to the river, the results could be hugely gratifying.

Odie surveyed the hillside and spotted the glimmer of movement that made the hairs on his arms stand on end. On a trail at the top of a wall of rhododendron he spied an ATV rider. After twenty-five years of running this gorge he knew exactly who it was: Frankie Hanks.

Frankie was of special interest to Odie. He was one of those people whose lifelines were woven through the fabric of his own. One day Captain Jack Stueben called him out of the blue and asked him if he knew the man and indicated he was a person of interest or POI. Jack told him he might be linked to the people who fragged him in Iraq and to let him know if he ever surfaced.

But Jack was not the only strand on which Mr. Hanks dropped into Odie Larson's world. He suspected Big Jane's beau might be associated with him somehow but he could not be sure exactly how as the information game via gossip at Moose Humps, the local tavern where he used to spend his evenings before he got into tango.

There were several rafts floating near him as he pulled out his cell phone and began texting a message to his crippled friend concerning the appearance of the POI. His sixth sense continued to tell him there was something wrong. When he finished his message and hit 'send', he surveyed the group of rafts surrounding his big green canoe.

The young Mennonite couples were the closest; Jose and his family were off to his left and the boat with only one couple was fast approaching as all the rafters entered a mile-long section of slow-moving water called The Doldrums. Peering downstream he could see Big Jane and a couple rafts a half mile away.

He worried that the Nelson Brothers were still nowhere in sight and felt the wrath of Big Jane coming on like storm clouds at the end of a hot summer day. He didn't like to see Janey angry even if he was not the object of her ire.

When a young lady in the Mennonite raft inquired about who he could possibly be talking to out here in the wilderness he seized the opportunity to help out his fellow river guides and also engage in one of his all-time favorite pastimes: storytelling.

By now the group of Hindis and the lawyers from Philadelphia had drifted into their midst. He could see Mr. Black at the top of the eddy just coming into view and still no sign of the surfing duo.

Taking off his sunglasses and looking the woman straight in the eye, he said, " I'm with the PA Bureau of Environmental Surveys and I'm here counting oo-bird nests." His eyes twinkled slightly as he turned his gaze from her to the other rafters surrounding him as if to let them know he was talking to all of them, inviting them all to partake in the conversation.

"What is this "oo-bird?" one of the Indian men asked, "I am educated in ornithology and am not aware of this occurrence or the name."

With a straight face Odie replied, " The oo-bird is very rare, the male of the species is called the oo-oo bird. He's a robin-sized creature with two-inch long legs and four inch long testicles; when he lands you can hear him yelling, 'ooh,ooh-ooh, ooh.!'"

There were chuckles from the rafters which seemed to act as magnet to lure other rubber boats from the expedition into a small floating island.

Jose asked in a loud voice, "Have you ever heard of the Fug-aw-wee Indians?"

The Fug-aw-wees were well-known to almost every loud-mouthed jerk from New York City, at least one of whom was guaranteed to be on a whitewater trip in the Lehigh Gorge on any given day. If Odie would have played into the joke, Jose would eventually tell him the fictional Fug-aw-wees were always lost and asking, "where the fug are we?"

"No, " Odie replied, stonefaced, "I'm just interested in finding the female oo-bird, have you heard of them?" He scanned the faces around him and he could see they were interested and a slight smile breached his lips.

Someone from the crowd of eight or nine rafts called out, "No."

"The female is called the oo-ahh bird. She's a three-pound bird that lays a five pound egg! You can hear her in the late spring laying the egg crying, 'ooooooooooooh!' an' when she's done she cries, 'AAAAAAhhhhhhhhhhhhh!'"

All the ladies laughed at this, heartily, and it was at this moment that Odie knew he had their full-fledged attention. Out of the corner of his eye he could see the Nelson Brothers stroking furiously with their paddles to catch up with the rest of the trip, certain their leader would be steaming mad. Mr. Black had his arm slung over a tube of the raft occupied by the young Chinese girls, conversing in Cantonese and Mandarin to all of them. Vicki's eyes gleamed with delight at his attention.

"Now today it just so happens is the first day of side-legged mountain creature mating season, " Odie spoke, in a voice loud enough to be heard by all but modulated so as not to appear to be yelling.

His tone was serious, yet the twinkle in his eyes assured almost everyone he was speaking in jest. "Side-leggers are real mean and vicious because they have a mating season once every five years and the mating season only lasts for three days....you'd be mean and vicious too if you could only mate once every five years for three days!"

More chuckles from the wetsuit –clad tourists, all of whom now were paying close attention to Odie and his every word.

"Now back in the fifteen hundreds when this land was first being settled the Spanish were up here trapping oo-birds and taking them back to Spain for a strange sexual cult that existed during the Spanish Inquisition. Lord knows what they were doing with those birds back then but the local Indians, who are known to this day as the Bingunknees Indians, were in a world of hurt owed to the depletion of their main food source by the Spanish trappers."

Odie scanned the entire cast of characters in his floating auditorium and continued laying it down thicker and heavier, " The Bingunknees, who were called the Bingunknees because they had a real tight hamstring in their legs an' when they would run the hamstring would tighten-out and pop and make a sound like, 'bing, bing, bing.' And when the settlers came here and heard that binging sound they thought it was coming from their knees so they called them the Bingunknees Indians. Now the Bingunknees were starving because the trappers were killing the Nareware Buffalo while they were busy catching oo-birds. The Nareware Buffalo were ideally suited to the hunting needs of the Bingunknees because they were deaf and they were the only animals that couldn't hear the Bingunknees

Indian warriors sneaking up on them with their, 'bing, bing, bing' giving them away all the time."

Seeing that the Nelson Brothers were taking a rest now that they'd caught up to the rest of the group and that the gathering of rafts were listening to his every word like he was Santa himself talking about his Christmas exploits and his friend the Easter Bunny, Odie lit into the rest of his story with gusto.

"Now that the Spanish trappers had nearly wiped out the Nareware Buffalo, Chief Tomochichi, the chief of the Bingunknees, had his warriors build the Bingunknees Indian Let-Go-By, a tall wall on the side of the river, this river, above a very nasty rapid called 'Staircase Rapids'. The only way, back then, off the Pocono Plateau and into the Lehigh Valley and the settlements beyond, for the trappers and traders, was by the river. When canoeists came up to the wall and didn't give the Bingunknees Indians all their food then the Bingunknees would throw rocks from on top of the wall and sink the canoes and the settlers would die in the rapids ahead. If the settlers gave up their food, the Indians would let them go by, hence the name."

"The Let-Go-By would still be standing today if it weren't for a man named Old Wild Bill Hickory, the first-gosh-darn-human-being-ever-to-be-invented, side-legged mountain creature trapper extraordinaire and the only man who swam down the mermaid Mama Minyata and took her pearl-handled shark's tooth knife. Now he fell in love with Pocono Pocohontas, the most beautiful Bingunknees Indian ever who could make a mountain lion purr with one softly spoken word and turn a grizzly bear into a teddy bear with a smile from her beautiful face."

Jose's stepson asked, incredulously, " How can you say that without taking a breath?"

"I can be long winded at times, " Odie answered, then continued with his story, "now, Wild Bill Hickory fell in love with Pocono Pocohontas but Chief Tomochichi, the chief of the Bingunknees forbade the marriage unless Wild Bill gave him the cash equivalent of 500 side-legged mountain creature skins. With that ultimatum Wild Bill came up with a plan to kill nearly all the side-legged mountain creatures and get them down the river to Philadelphia where he could sell them and buy the Indian princess."

"Wild Bill was a little guy, " Odie said, the group of rafts now tightly packed around his green canoe and all the customers were leaning over the edges of their boats to listen, "standing only three foot two inches high he was a highly misunderestimated individual, a very sneaky guy and he knew a lot of things other people didn't. For instance, he knew that when no one was coming down the river the Bingunknees Indian warriors had a stash of dried rhododendron leaves and when they smoke them something magical happened to them: whenever they threw rocks the rocks would go straight up in the air and disappear into the heavens and they would all laugh and laugh and laugh."

"The women Bingunknees didn't like their men hanging out at the Let-Go-By all the time but that's another story, but anyway, there was always one Indian who didn't partake of the smoke so as to be ready for a canoe coming down the river. "

"And Wild Bill knew something else, he knew that Martians, " Odie said but was immediately interrupted by Mr. Black who had floated into the storytelling session with his arm still hooked on Vicki's raft.

"Martians, " Mr. Black said with a voice that boomed, "now I know you're lying."

"Yep, Martians," Odie reaffirmed, unphased by the dark boat heckler, "he knew they used to suck up Lehigh River water and sell it throughout the galaxy because Lehigh River water was like alcohol on Saturn and Venus and a whole bunch of other planets. So Wild Bill came up with a plan and he and his friend, Alligator Magee, went and killed all the side-legged mountain creatures, more than 500, and then he convinced all the settlers to build canoes to take his skins down the river which were so heavy only one could fit in each canoe. The settlers were worried about the Indian Let-Go-By but Wild Bill told them he was going to destroy it, so the settlers formed a chain of boats so long it took three days for them to pass by any one place."

"Meanwhile, Old Wild Bill Hickory went upstream to the Martian Landing Pods, which are these right here, " Odie said as he pointed to three one hundred foot concrete foundations for an old railroad bridge that had burnt down a hundred years ago. The massive pillars stood like ancient titans bracing against the current in perpetuity in the middle of the river.

Most man-made obstacles on the river had several names, usually one logical or factual name, like the factual name for this place was 'Three Pillars', and a few fictional names, such as the Martian Landing Pods in reference to Odie's story or the 'Invisible Bridge' suggesting that there really was a bridge there but no one could see it. Further downstream a gas pipeline spanned the river and was known by nearly everyone as the motorcycle bridge inferring, falsely, that motorcycles used it to cross.

Continuing with his tale, Odie spoke, his audience still listening with rapt attention, "Wild Bill hid in the rhododendron bushes on a full moon and waited for the Martians to land on top of the central pod and he climbed up there and he tricked the Martians while their hose was sucking up the Lehigh River water, and he tricked them into getting out of their ships and riding on the poisonous caterpillars and the giant butterflies, but that's a different story. Well anyhow, Wild Bill got in one of their ships, which only he could do because he was so small and the spaceships were really small on the outside but giant on the inside. And figure out how to steer the ship and how to fly it and he flew it right into the Bingunknees Indian Let-Go-By, right into the Indians' dried rhododendron leaf stash and it caught on fire and started smoking and for three days there was thick smoke surrounding the Let-Go-By and it was at that time that Alligator Magee led the chain of canoes down the river, through Staircase Rapids, past the burning Let-Go-By, past a hundred smoke inhaling Bingunknees Indian warriors throwing rocks and laughing as the rocks all went up into the heavens. And the settlers in the canoes laden with the side-legged mountain creature skins laughed too as they floated pass the wall safely. They were so glad when they made it through the canyon of the Lehigh River Gorge that they built a town there and they named it 'Mauch Chunk' which in the language of the Bingunknees means 'burning Let-Go-By rocks going straight up.'"

The tongue twisting tale teller saw Big Jane holding her paddle perpendicular from way downstream indicating it was time to go and Haffie stroking furiously in her direction. He knew it was time to end the story so he looked at his audience and said with a tone of finality, "And that's how the town of Mauch Chunk got its name."

With that line people started snapping out their trances as if they'd been given the proper signal from their hypnotist. There was a rustling of paddles and squishing sounds as wet-suit clad butts slid agains rubber tubes. Then there was the sound of hands clapping, not a rousing applause but enough to make Odie blush with pride for he loved telling his story. He never considered himself the greatest river guide but he did pride himself on being able to tell a good story at a key time that helped his fellow guides escort their charges down the rapids with a greater degree of safety since they were all together in a group.

Not everyone was so inclined to hurry on down the river and they pleaded for more. Odie complied not wanting the rafts to all charge into the next rapid in a bunch.

"Well," he said, feigning reluctance but barely concealing a huge grin, "not many people know this," there were several chuckles from the paddlers, "but side-legged mountain creatures were eventually tamed and became the prime source of beef exported from the Poconos. Most people think lean beef has something to do with the fat content in the meat but it is actually derived from steepness of the hillside the critters are grazed on. So you know there is no such thing as 90% lean because the cows would fall right off the cliff! But it does make it easy for the farmer to harvest his cattle because all he needs to do is park his truck at the bottom, shoot the cow and hope it lands in the back."

"In 1937 the Bingunknees sued the Federal Government and won a hundred million dollars in a lawsuit which they used to build this here railroad track. " Odie held out his left hand to indicate the railroad grade which was easily visible now on the left bank of the waterway. " On Saturday nights the Indians will board their train on the motorcycles and ride it into the town of Mauch Chunk where they also own the supermarket. When the train arrives in town they ride off in their dirt bikes, surrounding the grocery store, all the while shooting flaming arrows into it. When it gets burning real good they run in inside and tie up the cashiers and haul off as much frozen food as they can and get back on the train and ride it back to their village where they cook their food and drink around a bonfire. Carpenters in town always have work, the cashiers are set free and the event has become a big tourist attraction."

"Okay, let's move it." Mr. Black said, his arm now unlatched from its hook on Vicki's boat, reassuming his role as sweep guide on a whitewater rafting trip through the Lehigh River Gorge.

Jose's wife said, "Wow, Jose, they even hired a real story teller to accompany us."

When Cassie and Tiresias paddled past Odie's canoe the hairs on his arm stiffened once again. Putting his sunglasses back on he stared at them with interest. The woman seemed to him to be agitated but Tiresias was totally serene, taking long deep paddlestrokes with his paddle and seeming to truly relish each one, a feeling Odie could understand. He often did that before he deployed or right after he returned from a long absence.

If something were wrong, he told himself, there was nothing he could do about it until he had some sort of clue as to what might occur. He resolved to keep an eye on the pair, maybe he could be of assistance to Big Jane if anything was to happen.

CHAPTER NINE

    Catching a fast current the retired river guide maneuvered his boat through the heap of boats, passing them as if they were standing still. Twenty years of river running experience taught him how to find the fastest moving water and to avoid the eddies where the water was actually moving upstream. Now ahead of the array of rubber boats, Odie paddled on alone.
    A kingfisher dropped off a tree branch above the water, swooped down in a huge arc crying, "kirr-kerr-kee-dee," as it went.
    A mile later he was at Lock #5 where he hoped to take some photographs of hummingbirds before the noise of the rafting trip disturbed the general stillness of nature.
    The lock was a ruin, abandoned after America's experiment with a lock and canal system to transport heavy freight along the waterways of the eastern seaboard. The heavy freight in this instance was coal. Several years of heavy flooding in the 1860's made it too expensive to repair the old system and the young country poured its efforts into building a railway system, using locomotives instead of canalboats.
    The lock is located across from the place known as Gould's Hole, a large acre-wide rock shelf next to a large eddy in the river. This eddy is the deepest water found on the Upper Gorge of the Lehigh River and almost everyone takes a break here when traveling through this section of the park. Such is the popularity of this place among boaters, that it came to be called 'Lunch Rock'.

Odie watched the arrival of the rubber armada while sitting on a child-sized folding chair his kids used when they were young. His portable isobutane single-burner stove was heating water for tea. Haffie arrived first paddling one hundred yards ahead of the first raft so he would have time to play on a variety of waves in the tiny no-name rapid just before the eddy at Lunch Rock.

Like a playful river otter, Haffie moved from wave to wave, stopping just before each wave, pointing his kayak upstream and, with a flurry of paddle-strokes, dropped onto the wave and achieved equilibrium. Surfing back and forth on each wave, he would peel off and dart across the stream to the next one. When he finished with the last one, he gave a sigh and shot a wistful glance back at the wave, like a lover who has to leave his partner in bed in the morning to go to work.

The young guide turned into the eddy on the east bank of the river, using his momentum to propel his psychedelic-orange kayak onto the rock shelf. In two moves he popped his sprayskirt off the cockpit of his boat and leapt out of it. He pulled his boat about ten yards up the rock surface to make room for the twenty rafts that needed to park here. Half-heartedly he began signaling the leading rafts to join him on the ledge. As each raft got close, he jumped into the water and pulled it up onto the rock, greeting the guests with a huge smile and kind words.

By this time, he and Fullie were in an aggressive competition for the attention of the young ladies on the trip. Haffie had one picked out and gave her raft special attention, making a big show of getting her boat so far onto the rock surface she would not have to put a foot into the water. He took her paddle, bowed and motioned with an extended arm towards the open space of the rock ledge.

Soon people were busy opening plastic twenty-gallon barrels to get at their lunches.

Odie's tea water boiled and he was now sipping tea. He watched Haffie with amusement and nostalgia. He was thinking how that used to be him, nearly twenty years ago, before life swept him away into the role of father and warrior, before Afghanistan and Iraq. How different those places were from here, he thought, the violence of the desert and the peaceful tranquility of the river. Now that he was back, the war seemed something from a history book. However, he knew it was not. The war was a part of him, he lived it...was still living it. He thought about his friend, Captain Stueben, now a cripple in a wheelchair.

Odie looked again to the other side of the river where the rafts were still coming into the eddy. Most of the rafts were parked on the shore. Fullie and Haffie were in all out competition for the attention of the girls on the trip; juggling apples, bananas and buckets, trying to see who could be the biggest, most skillful clown.

Odie smiled again, a small wistful smile. He was happy to be here, he thought, back on the river, his river, where he belonged. He was thankful that he was all in one piece and still a part of his kids' lives...that he still had Big Jane. As long as he and she were on the river together this was enough for him. He thanked God while he sat there on his yellow folding chair, on the west bank of the Lehigh River, watching Mr. Black and Big Jane pull into the eddy at Gould's Hole behind the last raft.

Cassie and Tiresias' raft was the last to arrive. Haffie and Fullie ran down to drag their boat so far onto the rock ledge that both were standing on a hard surface when they exited the rubber dinghy. Big Jane busied herself talking to the guests who were impressed with her leadership abilities and her job as an E.M.T. Mr. Black stayed in his kayak during lunch, preferring instead to work on his attaining abilities.

Attaining is the opposite of river running. River runners go downstream, attainers go upstream like salmon. Attaining is a sport limited to full-length kayaks. A short playboat like Haffie's would not have enough contact with the water to go upstream. To move against the current, a kayak must be designed to go fast, like Jane's boat or Mr. Black's.

Haffie and Fullie's kayaks were short, wide kayaks, designed for surface and subsurface stunts in even the slowest of currents. They were strong and heavy, constructed of thick plastic to slide against rocks.

Mr. Black's and Big Jane's kayaks were long and slender, made of a combination of Kevlar and graphite composite materials to make them strong and as light as possible.

Mr. Black kept himself busy moving from one eddy to the next trying to find his way back up the river. It is a slow process but it provided Mr. Black the physical and mental solitude he needed after this morning's episode. Physical solitude meant there would be no customers or other river guides; mental solitude meant there would be no other thoughts going through his brain only how he was going to make it up the next nautical incline to another eddy.

Mr. Black was not normally a people person. It was better that he found things to do to keep him away from the guests. He could be friendly on the water but, on dry land, his dark side would roll over the joyous atmosphere of lunchtime like storm clouds on a sunny day.

Socializing with the clientele is not a requirement river guides have to fulfill. A river guide is responsible for getting people from the launch point to the disembarkation area and that is all. If they decide to entertain the customers that is an added bonus and something most river guides are good at doing.

River guides are creatures of the water and as likely to love a person as to hate them, just as the river is capable of providing the grandest of thrills and drowning a person at the same time. True river guides are not people, they are a species all their own, born to run the river and never happy until they find it.

Odie watched Cassie and Tiresias as they disembarked and carried their gear to a secluded end of the rock. He watched them unload their lunch barrel and spread a blue and white quilt on the ground. Cassie took a pair of shoes out of a small velvet bag. Tiresias took out a camp stove like the one Odie used to boil tea water. He set a pot on it and filled it with water. Odie saw the other man stuff some leafy green vegetables in the water.

While the water was coming to a boil, Cassie took out a plastic shopping bag and removed three greeting cards from the bag. Each card, when opened, played a song.

The couple shared a passion for Argentine Tango ever since they first met nearly twenty years ago. Tiresias worked as a forecaster on Wall Street and Cassie was a waitress at a well-known Greek restaurant.

When the water boiled, Tiresias added more poison hemlock and turned the flame down to a simmer.

Walking over to Cassie where she stood on a smooth patch of ground, part stone, part sand, near to the edge of the woods, he opened the first card and took her hand as the song began to play. They danced to the song, La Cumparsita, a tango classic, accompanied by the sounds of the river, streams of tears running down Cassie's cheeks.

Across the river, Odie saw the couple dancing and watched in awe. He recognized it in an instant as Argentine Tango, the same dance he had been learning at the request of his friend, Captain Jack Stueben. He was too far away to hear the music emanating from the computerized greeting cards but he could tell by the way they embraced and moved around each other that it was definitely tango. This was the first time he had seen it performed in the outdoors and outside of a dance hall.

His thoughts drifted from the river to that world of concrete and machines.

Odie did not realize the enormity of the request his friend asked and how long it would take before he could even achieve proficiency in this dance. He had no dance training prior to accepting the task but was certain at the time that he could learn how to do it in three or four months. It had been two years and he was just beginning to feel stable on the dance floor. He was told many times, as he went to tango workshops and practice sessions, called practicas, that it takes five years for a man to learn how to lead Argentine Tango. He realized now that this was true.

Throughout his education in dancing he was inundated with brutal lessons in intimacy, on how to be close to women. He was overwhelmed at first. He had a difficult time not getting aroused when a beautiful woman took him into close embrace. Initially, he felt certain his dance partners were trying to seduce him. He realized later that the women came to the milongas to dance, not for sexual conquests. In two years he had not received one single offer to take the dance further than the dance floor.

How strange, he thought, that this dance followed him out onto the river. Odie marveled at how some themes seemed to run through his life, whether or not he chose to seek them out, the themes found him. There is no escaping tango, he said to himself and laughed aloud.

The entire crowd of rafters were now watching as the two moved around each other in close embrace, Cassie's feet tracing little circles in the sand, kicking between her lover's bent knee, twirling on the ball of one foot, tears running in torrents down both cheeks. Half of the women were cooing as they stared in wonder, with envy that Cassie had such a devoted lover.

After the first dance, Tiresias carefully picked up the card, closed it and put it back in a white envelope. He opened the second card, walked over to Cassie and took her into close embrace.

Odie watched with heightened interest. He took note of how the man went to the woman and offered his left hand to her by extending it out to the side, fingers pointing skyward. Cassie placed her right hand on his, hanging it there as she would a jacket on a coat rack. Tiresias moved his chest to hers and slipped his right arm around her back, placing his fingers just beneath her right shoulder blade. He let twenty seconds of the song pass as he waited for her breathing to synchronize with his. Her tears slowed to a trickle as she placed her wet cheek against his, her eyes closed to focus all her attention on the signals coming from her partner's diaphragm. When he was sure she was in 'tango trance', Tiresias began to move, walking her around backwards, in circles, turning around her in clockwise, and counterclockwise, movements.

When the second song ended, Tiresias went over and poured the tea into a huge mug, adding a little cold water to make it drinkable. He downed it all in one long gulp. He walked back to Cassie and opened the third and last card, the one titled "Una Emocion."

Cassie wailed, trying hard to concentrate on her lover's last dance but she could not, so he held her as she cried uncontrollably, kissing her wet cheeks, whispering in her ear, "It's all right, lamb chop, it's all right."

After the song ended, Tiresias put away all the gear. He took a rolled up towel out of their clothes bag and went over to their overturned raft, its black-rubber bottom hot and dry after being in the sun for the last fifteen minutes. He laid his cancer-ridden body down for the last time, his head propped up by the towel as if he were taking a short nap.

Big Jane headed over to Cassie to make sure she was okay.

Jane had no interest in the dance and had no idea that Odie was learning the tango, that this was the reason he began disappearing three and four nights a week, just before they divorced.

Cassie saw her coming towards her and managed a weak smile, using the back of her fist to wipe her now bloodshot eyes.

"That was so beautiful," Cassie said, as she focused on drawing the trip leader's attention away from her dying husband. She quickly composed herself and instinctively moved to protect the intentions of her dying soul mate.

Jane smelled something awful as she drew near, the smell of poison hemlock was not the most pleasant of odors.

Cassie grabbed her by the arm and asked, "Can you show me what it's like inside your kayak? We've done this trip so many times I think I'd like to try one of your boats next."

Big Jane was glad to move away from the acrid aroma. They both moved to the water's edge where Jane's black kayak sat.

The dance over, Odie decided to paddle over to the other side of the river and talk to the tango couple.

Haffie and Fullie were busy imitating professional wrestlers, doing body slams and back flips on an overturned raft which is springy and very much like a trampoline. Most of the crowd were now fully engaged watching the shenanigans of the two young river guides and only Vicki Lee was paying attention to Mr. Black who was almost out of sight as he moved slowly upstream.

Odie pulled his canoe onto the shore, near his ex-wife's boat. He had questions for Cassie and he waited for a chance to enter into the conversation.

He didn't talk too much to Jane since the divorce although their paths crossed frequently. They used to have intimate conversations when they were married, now their talk was dry and devoid of intimacy.

When he first started dancing, he could not tell her about tango. Although he never cheated on her while they were married, he found himself tempted many times and somehow managed to exit several situations with his promise to be faithful unbroken. He felt guilty as hell. He knew it showed, but he would not tell her about tango. He was not even sure back then, when he took his first lesson, that he had not betrayed her in some way. He knew she didn't need to hear him say it, they had been together long enough that each of them knew instinctively what the other was thinking. He had been thinking he was some sort of philanderer, he just didn't know what kind.

If the Army Ranger felt any qualms about being near his ex-wife, he never let it show. War had hardened him. He witnessed too many life-changing events. Events that happened a lot quicker than a divorce and had far more devastating consequences.

Deep down, he was angry, not because she wanted him out of the house or that she had a boyfriend; he was angry because it affected the kids. It pained him to see the kids wake up in her house and have to come to his house for breakfast. They were handling it okay, he thought, and beyond that nothing mattered except his 'tango' promise to Captain Stueben. Such was the bond between wartime comrades, bonds often greater than marriage vows.

"You and your friend dance well together," Odie said to Cassie just as she was running out of questions to ask Big Jane, making a poor attempt at feigning interest in learning how to maneuver one of the most unstable contraptions ever invented.

"Thank you," Cassie replied gratefully, turning towards him, she asked, "do you dance tango?"

When Odie replied, "Yes," Big Jane's jaw nearly dropped to the floor. She is jealous, he thought, and she does a lousy job of hiding it.

"I usually go to Firehouse, in New Jersey," he said, "or to New York City. I'm just learning," he added, a little sheepishly.

He looked to Jane. He could see she was flabbergasted...and angry.

"Where are you taking the girls on vacation?" Jane interjected, abruptly, with intended rudeness, suddenly transforming from fearless leader to an ordinary woman, a curious, jealous and angry ordinary woman. She turned her back to Cassie, much to Cassie's relief, and faced Odie, her fists clenched on her hips, her bent elbows pointing outwards, like thorns on the stem of a rose.

Cassie slowly walked away from the couple.

Odie replied, "I talked to Hannah this morning and tried to tell her we won't be doing the Moose River Bow trip up in Maine but she has her heart set on it, and, you know how it is with her, once she makes up her mind there's no changing plans."

"Well," Big Jane said, "you shouldn't make promises and break 'em. Yeah, she's strong willed, you need to talk to her about coming home late," she said, changing the subject, "I don't like it."

"Janey Ann," he said, using the name her mother gave her because he needed to disarm her, to calm her down and make her accept what he was about to say.

"She's eighteen, we raised her to make good decisions, now we gotta sit back and hope she makes it home alright." Then he threw in the clincher, the one thing most parents like to forget when confronted with raising their own child: their past. "Remember when we were skinny-dipping at the drinkin' dam at four in the morning, you were preggo with Hannah and you had two beers? You were eighteen years old."

Once he said it, he knew he shouldn't have. He touched a nerve when he mentioned one of the few times she gave in to the temptation of alcohol while nurturing her baby. Her motherhood was being affronted and her temper riled, her face blushed, not with aplomb more like a bomb…ready to explode.

"It was just TWO BEERS! And I…" she blurted out in a voice so loud everyone turned their heads, except Tiresias. The Nelson Brothers stopped mid-bodyslam, realized they were in competition for the group's attention and kicked it up a notch to trans-raft body-slamming…with their shirts off.

Odie tried unsuccessfully to cut her off, he knew the rest of the rant by heart.

"…and I'd like to see you have a baby!" she continued, her fists on her hips and her elbows bent, "and what about the time I had that cigarette? Huh? One cigarette in nine months, when are you going to let it go?"

"I'm not judging you, Janey Ann," he said, talking her back down from the proverbial cliff she was in danger of jumping off and into a tantrum, which always ended badly. "I'm not judging you, I'm just saying Hannah is going to be okay, she'll be alright, I'll talk to her, I'll talk to her."

Big Jane's cheeks lightened when she heard what she needed to hear. He was obeying.

He knew she would not like the tango thing and, at this moment, he was glad he didn't tell her. He felt anger. To him, it seemed she did not want him having fun during their entire marriage. However, Big Jane was a force to be dealt with…and respected, like the river. She was the mother of his children, he reminded himself.

Sometimes, the river, like a thunderstorm, forces a person to cope with elements they would avoid if they were somewhere else. In hindsight, he wished he hadn't seen the couple dancing, he had no desire to relive the pain of his divorce with Jane. That was the price he paid for keeping his 'tango' promise and he was going to keep on paying that price, as long as he stayed here on this river with his ex.

For the first time since his divorce, he was glad he was no longer married to Her!

With silent resolve, like a beaten fighter, he turned to leave the ring and pushed his green canoe into the stream. He peeled out of the eddy and decided to follow Mr. Black's cue, heading back up the river.

Attaining in a canoe was not possible for Odie, he had neither the skill nor the right canoe for such an endeavor. However, he needed to burn off a lot of steam and this was the best way to do it.

Mr. Black was just coming back into view. When he got closer, Odie abandoned his quest, feeling self-conscious and a little embarrassed in front of Mr. Black who was an expert at this aspect of kayaking. He felt that the dark man behind the sunglasses was laughing at him for paddling like an old man. It was true, he told himself. He even felt old. Plunging his wooden paddle into a strong current on the aft side of his boat, he leaned it sideways and pulled hard against the flow, whipping his canoe around 180°. With a flurry of paddle strokes, he headed down river. Winded and wheezing, he breathed a huge sigh of relief once he had his back to the people on the shore.

CHAPTER TEN

    Odie didn't have the urge to look back until he floated at least a quarter of a mile down the long eddy after Gould's Hole. A small breeze blew his canoe off its heading and was caught sideways in the wind. One of the many drawbacks of a canoe versus a kayak is how it responds to the wind. Kayaks are virtually immune to the effects of a strong blow but canoes are extremely susceptible and very difficult to maneuver, even in the slightest breeze. Once the canoe was broadside to the air stream, a canoeist needed to use many stomach muscles to force the bow back into the wind.

    Odie had a lot of stomach but he no longer had a lot of stomach muscles. Although he was a Ranger in the Army Reserves for twenty years, his job as a telecom specialist did not require him to climb mountains loaded with gear and ammo. More often than not, a helicopter or some other air transport dropped him off at his post and picked him up when it was time to leave. In addition, he had been home for more than two and a half years and a six-pack a night was no way to develop a perfect abdominal 'six-pack'.

    When the flurry blew, he didn't try to fight it, he let it take him around when he happened to catch site of Big Jane, signaling with her paddle, asking him to stop.

    River guides use their paddles to signal long distances, up to a mile or as far as the signaler's and signalee's eyesight permits. A paddle held vertically indicates 'All Clear' or 'Go'. A blade held horizontally above a boater's head indicates 'Stop'. A guide usually rotates the shaft so the blade catches the sun's reflection to catch another guide's attention. A paddle waved around in spiral indicates an extreme emergency! Two taps on the head indicates assistance is needed.

Once she got Odie's attention, Jane conveyed her desire that he come back with taps to her helmeted head, her elbows straight out to help the visual be understood at a greater distance. He stopped mid-turn and steered his canoe to the east bank where a slight upstream current and the breeze would quickly carry him back to Lunch Rock.

At the downstream end of the ledge, at least one hundred feet away and out of sight of the group, Big Jane met him, her face ashen white.

"What's wrong?" he asked.

"That guy who was dancing, he's fucking dead!" she replied.

Odie replied with disbelief, "What?"

"He's fucking dead!" she repeated. "And he's already stiff as a mother-fucking board, that's so weird. Jesus Christ. Jesus Fucking Christ. Fuck, shit, fuck, fuck, fuck!"

"Holy shit!" Odie chimed in, not knowing what else to say.

Jane continued to curse a few moments more before she began to calm down and eventually became silent. Odie thought about what to do but he knew the decision was ultimately Jane's.

"Did you do CPR?" he queried. It was unusual for an experienced E.M.T. to leave a victim so soon, after what, he assumed, was a heart attack or a stroke.

His ex-wife replied, "No! He's stiff as a board! I think he poisoned himself but the wife's acting like he did it accidentally, with whatever he brewed his tea with, only I don't quite believe her with all the crying she was doing earlier."

After a few moments, she added, as if in preparation for testimony she knew she would have to give later, "I could have gotten poisoned, too! Hell, no I wasn't going to give him mouth-to-mouth, even with a rubber duckie." She used the term she applied to the rubber mask a first aider can put over a victim's mouth to lessen the chance that any body fluids might transfer to the person delivering life-saving breaths.

With that said, she was suddenly calm. She knew what to do.

"Odie," she said, "you gotta stay here with the body and his wife. I need all four guides to get down the river today. The Nelson Brothers ain't worth a shit and M.B. is out of it since he got run'd over..." her voice trailed off. Odie knew she was seeing if he would go for corpse duty. He didn't like the thought of it after seeing so many in the deserts of Iraq after the initial invasion and during his second deployment back to the same country. However, he would do anything to help her.

"Okay," he said, "I get a full day's pay. You tell Steve O. he can give me cash or send it through the union." Steve O. was the owner of the touring company.

"Great!" she said and exhaled heavily, "I'll go to the top of the hill, call 9-1-1 on my cell and then we can get the body across the river. We'll leave the raft upside-down just the way he's laying on it now. That way we can just carry him up the bank while he's on top of the raft."

With those words she headed back to the group. All the people were milling around, not really sure what happened. There was no violence or convulsions, just a man lying down and not getting back up twenty minutes later.

Odie paddled his canoe up the eddy to the point where the dead man lay on the over-turned raft. When Big Jane came back down, they all got in their kayaks to escort the rubber dingy to the western bank of the stream, like some sort of bizarre Viking burial ceremony. Big Jane wrapped several rounds of rope around the raft and the body to keep it from slipping off. Odie leaned his canoe against the downstream tube and paddled on his free side. Big Jane and Mr. Black each jammed their kayaks under the front and back ends of the boat. Mr. Black, his back to the far shore, paddled in reverse. Big Jane, the raft and the corpse directly in front of her, paddled forward. Haffie and Fullie went directly to the far shore, thirty yards distance. Getting out of their boats, they jumped into the water to receive the funeral ship and keep it stable while the others dismounted from their crafts.

The ascent of the forty-foot embankment was a major operation, complete with multiple guidelines and pulleys. Getting the makeshift funeral vehicle over the edge of the steep hillside was the most grueling part of the whole ordeal. All five guides loaded the boat onto their backs and crawled over the edge, like giant ants bringing a trophy breadcrumb back to an ant colony.

At the top of the bank was a rails-to-trails bike path. It followed the Lehigh River from Whitestown to Easton where it joined the Delaware River and, from there, on to Bristol, PA, near Philadelphia. Here, there was a grassy area with a picnic table placed by park rangers to overlook the popular lunch spot.

All four river guides were grateful they did not have to stay with the dead man to wait for the ambulance to take it to the morgue. A wave splashed the former human being on the ride across the river and the body twisted and bent nearly into a sitting position in reaction to getting wet. They placed the body on one of the wooden benches of the picnic table, looking towards Lunch Rock. It still looked alive, as if it were merely reclining, its left ribcage braced on the edge of the table.

Odie stayed with the corpse while Big Jane paddled his canoe across the river to pick up Cassie. Once Cassie safely climbed the embankment, the trip leader scrambled back down, got in her kayak and went back to the rest of the guests who were waiting and wondering what they would do next.

Assuming the command position, once again perched on a raft and bracing on a paddle, she asked if anyone felt they could not continue. If so, she would arrange for them to wait with the deceased and his wife. Everyone agreed it was best to carry on and they all got quietly in their rafts.

Like George Washington's troops quietly crossing the Delaware River in the middle of the night, one cold Christmas day, many years ago, the group slipped into the water and drifted downstream with barely a sound.

Once the crew departed, Cassie sat on the bench next to her husband, across from Odie. The two endured a long, awkward silence before Odie finally broke the ice.

"You know," he said, "when I am at a milonga, I am never sure if I should say something in between songs when I am dancing with a woman. There is always this awkward silence, kind of like now." With that said, he looked at her sideways and smiled sheepishly.

A long, few moments passed before Cassie finally spoke, taking a deep breath and exhaling completely before she did.

"Y'know," she began, "it is just as difficult for the women to make it through those few moments between songs. We are hoping the man does not run off and not finish the tanda. It is an insult not to dance a complete tanda with a woman. The queasiness fades after awhile and you begin to relish those moments more and more as you dance tango. It means you are at a milonga." She tried to manage a smile but could not.

Odie was familiar with the terms she used but he rarely talked to other tangueras, as the women who dance tango are called. He knew a tanda was a group of tango songs, all in the same genre, or dance style, either tango, vals or milonga, and that 'milonga' could mean a place where tango is danced or a style of tango music and dancing. He knew it was impolite not to complete a tanda with the woman he invited out onto the dance floor.

Talking to Cassie revived memories of his many visits to his former first officer at the hospital in the Bronx. His superior officer loved to hear all about the difficulties he was having with this dance, from learning the Spanish terms to breaking through his fear of asking women for a dance. His friend would listen intently and then proceed to educate Odie on the numerous rules of social tango, as Argentine Tango was known.

Sometimes the incapacitated officer would grill him questions about who was at a certain tango event and what did they look like. Jack asked so many questions it made Odie wonder if there wasn't something else that interested the wounded man besides tango.

"Oh, look," Cassie said, "the wild strawberries are out." Getting up, she began walking up the bike path, searching for the tiny ripe berries. Bending over to pick each one, she walked on the trailside in the direction of Whitestown.

"Don't go picking any poisonous ones!" he warned. As he heard the words he spoke he felt very ashamed for his lack of sensitivity.

"I won't, you can be sure of that," she replied with more than a hint of anger.

Odie was relieved she was gone. Something about her made him feel uncomfortable. With her gone he could relax into the solitude of the canyon while they waited for the ambulance to arrive and take the body to the morgue. He wondered if there would be police officers. Anytime a person died, the local authorities were required to fill out a report on time and cause of death. He was certain the police would not question his ex-wife's word on how this man died. If Big Jane said the guy accidentally ingested poisonous herbs, then that's exactly what they'd write on their report.

He thought back to the old days, before cellular service covered this section of the park, when they had to paddle downriver to the truck and drive to a phone, or walk through the woods to the nearest house, two miles from where he now sat.

As Odie reminisced, he looked at the corpse and saw something that made his hair stand on end: the dead man was sitting with his belly to the table, his arms crossed and elbows in front of him, his vacant eyes staring in the direction of the river. Odie shut his eyes and reopened them...twice, but the scenery stayed the same.

"Hey, man!" Odie shouted, "We thought you died, man!" He looked up the old railroad grade for Cassie, but she was out of sight.

"I did die," Tiresias stated flatly.

The river guide stared at him, his jaw suspended in disbelief, his heart beating wildly. It seemed to Odie the air was colder on the side of his body nearest the apparition. Though he saw his fair share of dead bodies in Iraq and Afghanistan, he never experienced anything like this. Once, on a mountaintop in Afghanistan, he spent the whole night with the lifeless body of a young marine killed in combat. The corpse was left at Odie's bunker while his marine buddies continued to engage the enemy.

"I fucked up," Tiresias said.

"Shou...should I get Cassie," the canoeist offered, stammering uncontrollably, "I'll go get her."

"She cannot see me. I am dead to her now," the corpse said. "Stay!" he commanded, as Odie tried to get up, forcing him back down onto the bench with his demand. "I can't go until I say it out loud."

Odie asked, completely confused, "What?"

The animated cadaver explained, "I've made a big mistake. I cannot cross the river until I say it out loud, until I admit my mistake. I took my love for granted. I ended my life instead of letting it end itself. I was too proud of my love for her." Tiresias turned his whole upper-body to the left, in morbid fashion.

The deceased continued, "Life dealt me a humbling blow and I refused to learn from it. I could have stayed with my love. My love was the gift I was given and I chose to leave it of my own accord. I chose poorly and now...I...must go....back again..."

The dead man's body was suddenly as it was before, twisted, bent slightly, its ribs braced against the table in a seemingly painful position.

CHAPTER ELEVEN

    A half hour after leaving Odie at Gould's Hole with Cassie and the disenchanted, lifeless body of Tiresias, Big Jane was up to her eyeballs in the chaos that is No Way Rapid. Named for the lack of a clear and obvious route through the mile long turbulent section of rapids, with its wide variety and abundance of unique hazards, No Way, as it was called by the guides, was the devil's friend.

    The top section of the rapid, barely one hundred yards long, consisted of a large wide shoal located in the middle of the river. Shoals, while not dangerous themselves, become extremely hazardous when located above a particularly nasty stretch of rapids like this one. A shoal is a shallow patch of water where the current is thin, running over a small field of stones or a rock-shelf in a slender sheet. Immediately preceding the shoal, the current can be deceivingly strong, often causing a boater, especially a boater in a raft, to fall out or tip over.

    For a rafter to fall out on a shoal is almost always painful. They exit the raft into the shallow water, directly onto the small rocks or rock shelf. Usually the current drags them along the shoal, where, unable to find their footing, they enter deeper water. If the deeper water should be a dangerous rapid, their troubles are just beginning. Any injuries they sustained in the shoals get worse in the convoluted rapids.

    The river rushed to the left and right of the shoals at the entrance to No Way Rapid. The current going to the left of the shoals turned sharply towards the right bank and ran nearly straight towards it. The right-side course rocketed alongside the riverbank into a large boulder, protruding four feet out of the water at this river level.

Amazingly, very few rafts ever pinned on this rock. Rafts would hit it hard, usually sending bodies into the water, but they did not stick to it. The rock could be avoided if rafters were properly warned.

After this obstacle, a seemingly calm stretch of water ensued but this was merely an illusion. The pool between the rock and the main body of the rapids was about sixty yards long. Here, three smooth but strong currents carried rafters quickly into the jaws of the monster.

A small boulder-pile of car-sized rocks forced most of the river's flow to the east side of the waterway. With pent-up anger in its quest to the sea, the main force of water rushed back to the eastern bank, its energy translated into huge wave trains, violent whirlpools and disappearing eddies. A plethora of foaming whitewater figures sprung up immediately, denoting holes, hydraulics and breaking waves.

While most of the water now moved to the left side of the river, a third of it still rushed through a boulder field on the right. Here, there was enough current to carry a skillful crew of paddlers all the way to the bottom of No Way. There, they could join the main body of water once again. A skilled crew could do this, unskilled crews made it in but did not make it out unassisted.

The stream running down the left continued to create more whitewater obstacles until it culminated in a rock/water configuration known as No Way Chute. The name, No Way Chute, was deceptive, for it was not one chute but a chain of chutes arising out of an underwater boulder garden. The rocks impeded the main current almost entirely and diverted it to the right at a 90° angle.

Only one sluice was big enough to pass through at any one time. There were so many channels to pick from, a boater, traveling at the speed of the river, had very little time to make the correct choice. All the other routes either pinned rafts or violently forced them through a trough.

When a raft is squeezed through an opening between two rocks, injuries occur and people are tossed overboard. Things always go wrong here. A guide's job is to make sure nothing goes 'very' wrong.

Due to the unusual circumstances at lunch, Big Jane did not properly instruct her fellow guides on where she wanted them to set up safety points in the rapid. If she had, she would have made an animated point to Fullie explaining her desires. She did not want him sitting near the huge boulder at the end of the first section of No Way Rapid. She would have told him to sit on the eastern bank of the river, to the left of the obstacle, directing traffic into a large raceway to safety.

Fullie did not learn his lesson in Entrance Rapids, the lesson that Big Jane did not want him to sit near obstacles, that she wanted him to sit near smooth channels of water for rafts to pass through. He would suffer her wrath later.

Worse yet, Big Jane did not learn that she could not count on Fullie to do his job according to her wishes. She would suffer the wrath of the river, which was painful, swift and deadly.

She was floating to the right of the shoals when she spied the ambulance transport, carrying

Odie, the corpse and Cassie, on its way down the railroad grade to Coalport.

As she came around the bend after the shoals section, she saw Fullie, eddied-out behind the large boulder, waving rafts towards the left side of the river, both arms flailing frantically...people and paddles were in the water everywhere!

Jose's raft passed her as it made it around the shoals and was now heading toward the rock where Fullie was. Jose was in the front section of the rubber craft, one leg hanging out of the boat, his paddle ready to encounter rock obstacles.

"Getchyer goddam leg back in the friggin' boat! " Jane yelled to Jose, for the umpteenth time this day. "stay left, this side, this side, stay left!!!" She momentarily let loose of her kayak paddle, so it rested on top of the sprayskirt covering the cockpit of her kayak, so she could wave her arms at the rafters. She quickly picked up her paddle to affect a flurry of strokes that brought her to the position she wished Fullie had chosen earlier.

"Hey, fuckwad, right here!" she yelled to Fullie, her shrill voice piercing the sounds of the roaring rapids. When he looked her way, she shot him an angry glance, pointing to the spot where she was now sitting and displayed the proverbial finger. She pointed downstream with her hand.

Nearly three quarters of the rafts were now past this point and almost all were in trouble. She hoped to convey to Fullie that he needed to start rescuing the customers, but he totally freaked out when he looked at Big Jane, his brain shutting down.

All he could do was sit and watch. Great kayaker that he was, he was not a great river guide. This epiphany became apparent to him now and he sat paralyzed in the eddy behind the large rock at the bottom of the entrance to No Way Rapid, the complexity of the calamity being too much for his mind to fathom.

With a short, quick burst of paddle strokes, the trip leader's boat accelerated from zero to sixty in three seconds. She steered towards the troubled rafters, shouting audible directions to some and shoving the nose of her kayak into others, like a sheep dog barking and biting at the ankles its herd. She began the hopeless task of getting everyone back in their boats before the main body of the rapid began.

Haffie was working with the four rafts nearest him as he drifted into the swift current to the heart of the rapid. He tried to get everyone to follow him to the left side while assisting other boaters, verbally and physically, to pull swimmers into rafts and to bail rafts filled with too much water.

Fullie sat, still paralyzed, behind the large boulder, as Big Jane caught the attention of Mr. Black. He was coming around the bend, ahead of the last three rafts entering the shoals. She tapped her helmet three times quickly and waved her left arm towards Fullie. Mr. Black saw her and the carnage. He immediately abandoned his charges and propelled his narrow kayak towards the eddy where Fullie sat.

Shooting into the eddy, he nearly gored Fullie with the tip of his boat. Mr. Black pulled himself next to him and said, "Okay, you wank-headed bugger, you're now sweep guide," pointing upstream and making sure Fullie looked in the direction he was pointing, he said, "make sure you come down behind the last raft and no one is behind you!"

He didn't wait for Fullie to acknowledge that he understood. Mr. Black shot out of the eddy and into the current heading for a group of rafts where several people and paddles were in the water. He eyed-up four rafts just beginning their descent into the major part of the rapids. It was the girls from Fuzhou. Three of the girls were in the water, three were bent over the sides of the raft with arms extended, reaching towards their floundering friends. One girl held the only remaining paddle and was somehow managing to steer the raft effectively into the main flow of the current where it needed to be.

Like a mythical water-dragon, Mr. Black circled the boat, picking up paddles and tossing them to the young woman steering. She caught each with one hand and quickly placed it into the raft.

"Xie-xie, " she replied, swiftly and politely, with the Chinese word for "thank you," as she caught each paddle.

The young, Indonesian kayaker, maneuvered the stern of his boat underneath one young woman in the water while another was tossed onto the deck by a wave. Letting go of his double-bladed kayak paddle, he grabbed the raft's outer rope and held on. He reached for a third swimmer a split second before she was run over by another rubber monster. With a heave and a ho he deposited her into the raft. The girl on the back of his kayak bounded off with a squeal as the girl on his deck hit him in the head with his own kayak paddle, saving it from being swept away by the current.

"Xie-xie," the dark water-dragon said, beaming. He recognized the young girl who had fallen overboard at the beginning of the trip. His paddle flashed in the sunlight as he grabbed it.

Catching an eddy, he spun his boat around and shot it back out into the strong current with one swift paddle stroke. Like a ripple in the water, he was gone, off to help another raft.

Big Jane was at No Way Chute. Holding onto a rock barely jutting out of the water, she deflected rafters into the chute with her kayak as they drifted into her. Ignoring swimmers clinging to rafts, she held her position until three quarters of the trip passed through the chute. Jose's raft managed to sneak past her between the left shore and her kayak, with two rafts directly behind his.

He did not realize what was going on even as he watched it happen in slow motion. His raft turned sideways as he passed to the left of the woman in the kayak, his legs straddling the outer tube. With his peripheral vision, Jose could see two more rafts bearing down on his as they all went into uncharted waters.

The policeman from New York City saw his rubber bootie-clad foot slide between two small boulders, twenty-four inches beneath the surface of the raging river. It did not jam badly. He would still be unscathed if he had one more moment to slide it out of the water and back into the boat. However, he did not have one more moment and the raft's momentum, combined with the momentum of two more boats, immediately bent his leg until it snapped sideways at the calf, both lower leg bones breaking with a certain ,"snap."

His wife and stepchildren watched in horror as they heard bones breaking and saw Jose withdraw the mangled limb back into their rubber sanctuary from the angry jaws of the rapids.

Big Jane heard the sound of bones breaking and knew instantly what it was and to whom it happened.

Great, she said to herself, as she abandoned the channel where she forcefully averted rafts into the proper slot.

With a flurry of paddlestrokes, she was on the scene. She redirected the two rafts on top of Jose's into another passable channel. Hanging onto the rope running the perimeter of the injured customer's raft, she popped off her sprayskirt and climbed into the raft. Pulling her kayak into the raft with her, she spied the broken limb, winced and grabbed her kayak paddle. Giving the river guides' signal for STOP, she waited until Haffie, now in the calm pool at the end of the rapid, returned the signal in acknowledgement.

While everyone in the raft was still in shock, Big Jane employed her first aid skills. She produced several white cravats, triangular pieces of cloth used to splint broken limbs, from somewhere inside her lifejacket and began strapping the leg to a paddleshaft. Holding Jose as still as she possibly could inside a rubber raft floating down the last big waves of No Way Rapid, she steered the boat by voice command, issuing explicit paddling instructions to his stepchildren and wife, telling them when and on which side of the boat to paddle.

"Right side, back paddle, okay, now forward on the right. Back paddle on the left, okay, chill," the blond haired woman called while trying to keep her injured guest from rolling around inside the raft as the boat bounced off rocks and crawled over three foot waves.

Except for Jose, everyone made it through unscathed. Many swam several parts of the turbulent section of waterway. Mr. Black and Fullie worked like two well-trained sheep dogs, assisting boaters who were trying to haul in swimmers or bumping rafts with their kayaks at just the right moment to move a boat into a particular current that would carry the rafters safely around obstructions.

Haffie had most of the rafts in a group on the right side of the river near a small, sandy beach.

Big Jane guided her charges into the eddy on the upstream side of the small flotilla. She made eye contact with Mr. Black, then tapped her helmet twice with her open palm. Fullie hung his head and used the flat nose of his whitewater playboat to bump rafts into a tighter circle. Hoping to hide his shame, he made an aggressive effort to move the boats into a more compact group.

Jane and her second-in-command made their way upstream to the edge of the beach, out of earshot of the customers.

"I think I should stay with the bobbie," Mr. Black offered but Big Jane turned him down immediately.

"No," she said. "I'll kill Roger if I have to watch him fuck up again." She used Fullie's real name because she had a difficult time referring to him by his river name. A river guide's nickname is a term of respect and endearment, none of which she was feeling right now.

"I might kill NYPD, too, but customers we can always get more of, river guides we have to train and that's just too painful," she said, trying in vain to inject a little humor into the situation.

"MB, all jokes aside, I'm an E.M.T. I'm sure this guy'll sue Steve O. if we don't take super care of him. No, you take the trip but don't leave until I've contacted the county 9-1-1."

Mr. Black didn't put up much of a fight, preferring to avoid dead and injured persons, even more than African-American lawyers who escape to the Poconos for fun and frivolity.

Big Jane climbed the riverbank until she got high enough where she could place a call on her cell phone. Taking out her phone, she made the call and texted Odie. She let him know her situation and that she wouldn't be needing a ride. She thanked God out loud that there was so much cell phone coverage in this part of the gorge. If she had been on the lower section of Lehigh Gorge State Park, she would not have been able to make a call anywhere except at the launching areas.

Haffie and Fullie snapped her out of it when they appeared with a backboard and a pile of cravats to strap down the injured Jose. The embankment here was not so steep and they hauled the injured tourist up to the biking path in a few short minutes. Jane asked Mrs. Morales if she'd like to wait with her husband for the ambulance but Jose wouldn't allow it. He threw such a fuss that his wife just shrugged her shoulders, cast a sorrowful looked to the female E.M.T. and headed back to her children in the raft.

Jane explained to the guests that she was staying with Jose and that Mr. Black was now their trip leader. Although everyone's spirit was dampened by the recent, tragic events, they gladdened somewhat at the prospect of being led by the acrobatic and quite capable Mr. Black. He demonstrated his ability to assist them in times of trouble instead of performing stunts, like the forward guides, Haffie and Fullie. In addition, his British accent came in extremely handy, instilling confidence in the beleaguered crowd of tourists.

He had the entire group wish Jane and Jose, "good luck and God-speed."

"Hi-ho, off we go!" he yelled, as all the boaters dipped their paddles into the water and propelled their rafts downstream towards new adventures waiting ahead.

When the group was out of site, Big Jane turned to Jose, lying in obvious pain on a stretcher next to her, and said, "Wanna get high? You could probably use it, I'll bet, especially since I've got no morphine or other kinds of drugs to give you."

"What?" Jose asked in disbelief, not sure the pain was making him delirious. He had recreational drugs of his own, stashed in an inner pocket of his jacket. "Nah, I don't wanna smoke none of your hillbilly homegrown weed, I got something better."

The woman smiled at her patient's seemingly good spirits but could not resist the challenge.

She said, "Not better than the Afghan, hillbilly hash my ex brought back from the war, I'm sure."

Jose chuckled and jarred his leg, sending waves of throbbing pain running through him, like his very own turbulent river of agony. He barely squeaked out his reply, "Lay it on me sister........I guess the doctor is in."

CHAPTER TWELVE

The ambulance arrived to pick up Tiresias' corpse, Cassie and Odie. Driving on the old railroad grade alongside the river, they could see the rafting trip as it entered No Way Rapids, Odie's green canoe hanging out the back door of the vehicle.

At Coalport, Odie transferred the canoe to his van and followed the ambulance to the morgue at the county seat. The county sheriff questioned him briefly and soon he was on his way home. Cassie had to ride back to the tourist center with the sheriff and his aide so they could finish the paperwork associated with accidental deaths.

Unexpectedly happy to be moving at the speed of automobiles and not at the speed of a canoe on the river, Odie's thoughts traveled back to the couple dancing tango by the riverside. He thought once again of Captain Stueben and of his commitment to him to learn this dance. He had a strong urge to report a new tango adventure to his former first officer. He was beginning to feel that tango was sort of like therapy. He could feel himself starting to heal but could not explain how it was happening.

Today was a good day for it, he thought. Losing himself in the mesh of human bodies at a milonga would help him forget the events of the day and how much they reminded him of the war. He winced at the memory of Iraq and its desert tragedies, its car bombings and broken society. It made him appreciate the seeming normalcy here:

someone dies, an ambulance is called and now the body is at the morgue.

He wanted to escape those thoughts and a tango expedition would be just the trick. His desire to escape the contrast between life over there and life here, back in the States, was so strong that he no longer considered a two-hour trip to the large metropolises of New York City or Philadelphia a nuisance.

He decided he would head down to Philadelphia for a milonga beginning in the early evening and another milonga in mid-town lasting until the early hours of the morning. Tango dancers often danced until dawn.

Usually, he went to New York so he could visit the Captain. Today, he decided on a different direction. The two cities were equidistant from his perch in the Poconos and each had its own flavor of tango to offer.

He found the enormity of the Big Apple to be forgiving as its size offered a greater degree of anonymity. In New York City there were milongas and practicas seven days a week. A practica was much like a milonga. Here, dancers were allowed to work on the fundamentals of tango, often stopping mid-song to examine and discuss the dynamics of a particular movement. Practicing at a milonga was frowned upon and considered extremely offensive to everyone in attendance.

At a milonga, the experience of the crowd as a whole often amplified the experience of individual dancers. Therefore, an offense to the group was the greatest of all possible sins as it created the greatest number of victims. A collision could be forgiven, an intentional breach of the rules could not.

Lately he found his tango experiences in Philadelphia to be most rewarding. There, through its scant offerings of practicas and milongas, he found satisfaction and confidence in his dancing. He felt more comfortable in Philly than he did in New York City. He guessed this had something to do with the fact that he learned in New York City and arrived on the Philly tango scene with some proficiency dancing tango. The folks in Philadelphia did not experience him when he was a total klutz with two left feet the way he arrived in NYC.

Back at his house he ignored the cries of his overgrown lawn along with many other household chores and began packing for the long ride to tango. He removed his canoe from the top of his van and put it on a rack in his backyard.

He ironed a few shirts so he could change when he got too sweaty.

He packed his cooler taking several frozen water bottles out of his freezer where he had many stored to save on ice. He stacked them in a hard-shelled cooler picked up years ago on a canoe camping expedition to the backwoods of Maine and the Moose River with Big Jane and the kids. He also packed more than enough bottles of beer for the ride home. She would have given him a hard time about the beer, he mused, then packed two more for spite.

In the laundry room on the first floor he grabbed three clean t-shirts from a pile of folded clothes on top of the dryer. He snagged a pair of fluffy hiking socks from a basket on the floor. They provided the most comfort to his feet when he danced three to five hours at a stretch.

Upstairs, in a room where he had a weight bench set up for working out, he picked up a small blue gym bag packed in case he got 'lucky'. In two years of dancing this had not happened but that did not stop him from packing it anyway. Nor did it stop him from throwing a sleeping bag and some pillows into the back compartment of his van. He had removed the bench seat to make room for sleeping when he was too tired, or too intoxicated, to drive.

His van had been a blessing to him after his divorce. The last two years he had taken many tango trips and often found himself sleeping at a roadside rest area at 4 a.m.

Although he would never have opted for a dissolution of their marriage, he could understand Jane's confusion and emotional angst at his indifference and separateness. He knew from the start she would never understand about his promise to Stueben. He accepted, long before she decided to divorce him, that his marriage would be just another casualty of the wars in Iraq and Afghanistan.

If he could just continue to be in his children's lives and be near Big Jane, he thought, that would be enough for him.

Now there was something else happening in his life, alive and breathing, growing inside of him...it was tango.

Born in the latter half of the nineteenth century in the barrios of Buenos Aires and Montevideo, where young men from Europe, mostly from Italy and Germany, hoped to eke out a living on the frontier cattle ranches and fertile fishing waters of Argentina. Like two rivers coming together to form a new river, so too did the disparate cultures of this fledgling region meld together. Somehow, a slave population from Africa and an immigrant wave of Germanic and Latin men, managed to come together to create a thing of beauty and a paradox of complexity in a simplistic form of movement.

Argentina, like its northern neighbor, the United States, experienced a seismic transformation, going from a vast, untamed wilderness into an agricultural and industrial machine of the twentieth century. Like its northern cousin, that country had vast deployments of iron and lumber, creating railways and a huge shipping port in Buenos Aires. However, unlike the United States, Argentina lacked a population of women equal to the size of the many men working on fishing boats and cattle ranches in this young country. Most of the men were providers for their families back on the European continent and found comfort in the brothels of the city.

If a man desired to marry and make a life in the New World, his choices for marriage came from a very small pool of single women often forced to choose between prostitution and starvation.

At this time, a style of music was becoming popular with the local peoples in the barrios, or ghettoes, of Buenos Aires and Montevideo. The music came to be known as 'tango', based on rhythms brought from Europe, adapted by German immigrants to include an instrument known as the bandoneon, an accordion-type musical device, and sung by Italian balladeers. This music was extremely infectious with its unique blend of African and European rhythms, it was emotionally moving and very popular.

By the 1920s and 1930s, competition for the available women had become so ingrained into the local culture that a system developed where the men proved their worth by their ability to dance tango. A young man growing up at this time would be indoctrinated into the ways of the dance during his adolescence, at age eleven, the age when he typically started working for a living. For three years, he would only dance with other young men, to music played by live musicians at the brothels downtown. Only when they were ready to begin dating, at the age of sixteen, were they allowed to attend the milongas.

The poor young men of Argentina and Uruguay were not the only ones partaking of this dance, so too, were the affluent young men of the newly wealthy families of Buenos Aires who were sent off to school in Paris. Once there, they spread their passion and style of dancing in what would soon be known as 'The Forbidden Dance'.

Tango spread like wild fire around the world through the great metropolitan areas of that time: Paris, New York, Rome, Istanbul and London. This dance, once looked down upon with disdain in its home country as a disgraceful anomaly practiced only by the poor, became a source of national pride and began to be performed openly at all levels of society in Argentina.

Beginning in the 1940s, the right-wing, oligarchic government of Argentina tried to ban the tango gatherings as a means to prevent public assembly. For forty years the dance was forced to remain underground, where it festered like the sucker of a tree, cut down in its prime and not ready to stop growing.

In the late 1980s, tango burst through the dense undergrowth of the ailing oligarchy, like a flowing river that would not be constrained following the release of two musicals: Tango Argentino and Forever Tango.

The global appeal of Argentine Tango, still as vibrant as ever, if not more so, with its forced aging, like a vat of fine scotch, exploded back into its old haunts in Europe, Asia and the Americas, like plants in the desert after a heavy rain, intoxicating its supplicants with renewed vigor. It even found new footholds in places like Tokyo, Shanghai, Seoul and Singapore. It grew any place there was a large, international community, mostly near universities or densely populated cities like New York, London and Paris.

The international flavor of tango's participants was something Odie found very appealing. He liked being anonymous. Anonymity made it easier for him to venture forth into the world of dancing without a sense of embarrassment. He could never have done this in Whitestown, he mused, crossing the bridge over the Lehigh River, heading east.

He thought about how much he changed as a person since he started dancing tango. He entered the tollbooth at the entrance to the northeast extension of the Pennsylvania Turnpike, Rt. 476. The EZ-Pass light flashed yellow, then green, as he rolled through at ten miles per hour. In a wide sweeping turn around the entrance ramp, his scenery changed from towering trees to a magnificent view of the southern table of the Pocono Plateau.

In a half-mile he crossed over the headwaters of Hayes' Creek and said to himself, "What a beautiful stream," as he always did when he made his way 'off the mountain', as some locals liked to say, heading south to Philadelphia.

He crossed over all the streams emptying into the Lehigh Gorge from the east, including Drakes' Creek, Stoney Creek and the infamous Mud Run with its large concrete span of a bridge over its deep, rhododendron-covered canyon and Class VI rapids.

Before tango, he remembered, he was uncomfortable being near other people. Although he could be close to Jane he was never comfortable revealing his personal side, he always liked to control what she knew. He liked it when she revealed things about him he found pleasing but would clam up when she would point out his faults. Tango was teaching him how to feel more comfortable exposing his inner-self to the women who were his dance partners. He was learning, he thought, how to make a mistake and not agonize over the event so much.

The biggest hurdle Odie had to overcome in dancing was dealing with arousal. This was something he could not talk about to anybody, not even Jack Stueben. He was not comfortable talking about his sexuality. He thought he would be embarrassed if a dance partner looked down and made fun of a 'tent' growing in his trousers. This incident never happened, yet he worried about it often. So far, he had been lucky. After dancing with hundreds of women, he found that arousal occurred with less frequency. He was even able to take a woman into close embrace and remain 'respectful'.

In Argentine Tango, there are two types of embraces: open and close.

In open embrace, there is a space between the partners and it is easier to maneuver separately from each other, making complex movements easier to perform.

Odie likened close embrace to the Vulcan Mind-Meld. He saw the character, Spock, employ this hold on many Star Trek episodes he watched on TV as a kid. He was more relaxed now taking a woman into close embrace than he had been even six weeks ago. Finally, he was able to make some progress around the dance floor in this position. His first attempts at this posture resulted in a sensory overload that made it difficult to hear the music and think of what move he would do next.

Now, he realized, the best dances happened when a woman was able to move into and out of his embrace, open or closed, so he had the option to employ a wider variety of movements in his dance, making him a more interesting leader.

He found a tanguera was not just a visual delight but also a plethora of other worldly pleasures: perfume, soft hair, soft skin.

Learning Argentine Tango, he told Captain Stueben, was a foray into the jungle of femininity. Having dated only Big Jane and a few other girls before he married her, his experience with other women was limited to girls who were capable of doing hard work. He found the women in tango enjoyed their femininity and worked to exploit it to the point where it made his head reel. He was particularly susceptible to a number of perfumes but two stood out in his mind as the most sensual and somehow made him think of food.

Of late, he had been working on his connection to his partner. It took him nearly a year and a half but he finally decided a woman was a lot like an improvised explosive device, or IED. He never disarmed one of these dangerous creatures but he had been to many training classes and watched several times as military bomb squads disabled them. One thing he learned: he had to be very, very careful.

He began to appreciate how much less stressed he was after a night of dancing tango. He was now able to laugh about his mistakes on the dance-floor and even ignore them, so as not to interrupt the rhythm of the dance.

He found himself enjoying the moment of initial contact with his dance partner. When he looked at women as potential explosions, he was able to proceed into the embrace with the proper amount of caution and attention to the female psyche. She needed to know, he thought, that he was capable of leading her into motion as she walked backwards into an unseen crowd. Any indications leading her to believe something to the contrary would have an unraveling effect. She would become nervous, looking around for possible collisions, eventually her composure would crumble and he would be left holding the pieces, waiting for the song to end.

The last few milongas he attended, he received positive feedback from the women with whom he danced. They said his lead was clear, easy to understand, that he had a unique sense of musicality. They enjoyed his company.

Imagining his success, he thought he would soon be privy to a romantic interlude, in spite of what his crippled friend told him.

"Tango," Jack Stueben said, to his former charge, "is about sensuality, not sex. If you focus on sex you will miss out on the greatest benefit of the dance, your connection to the woman you are dancing with. That is what tango is all about: connection."

In a way, Odie thought, the Captain was right. His fantasies about having sex with a particularly good-looking woman from a prior dance, were gradually being replaced with fantasies about having good dances. He worried that these kinds of thoughts meant he was getting old.

Tango truly was torture, he thought, as he drove down the long, five-mile hill into the Lehigh Valley, the rolling countryside below, a geometric mosaic of farms and farmhouses. He hadn't had sex in over two years and here he was, driving two hours to learn this intricate and bizarre ritual. All the while he was supposed to suppress his arousal which definitely seemed like the most appropriate physical response to the situation. Maybe, he mused, he should have been going to a brothel and saving himself all this hassle.

As he entered the Lehigh Tunnel beneath Kittatinny Mountain, it occurred to him tango might be killing his sex drive. Tango was forcing him to look at women in an entirely different light. He was seeing them as partners in exercise, not just sex objects. He found himself immensely appreciative of a woman's efforts to execute her role with proficiency. A good partner, he thought, is like an asset to the team, a member of his squad, a fellow warrior in pursuit of perfection in this dance.

He found these thoughts worrisome. He feared someday he might lose his youthful attraction for the opposite sex and become an androgynous heap of passionless skin and bones.

Reassuringly, he told himself his embrace of women was as rewarding as ever...and becoming something more.

It was 'something more' because he worked so hard to achieve a perfect union with the dance partner, the same way two canoeists, paddling together in the same canoe, learn how to work their way through a difficult rapids section. However, he pondered, bursting out of the darkness of the tunnel and into the light of day, tango is with many partners and finding the right one to dance with, the one with the natural chemistry, was the purpose of this dance.

 He concluded that Captain Stueben was right. Connection was all that mattered and with that thought he gave up all his hopes for a sexual encounter. He discarded those hopes like so much extra baggage. He felt better. Relieved, lighter, like a great burden had been lifted from him. Tonight, he would focus on connection and nothing more.

 Once through the tunnel, a traveler is confronted by two merging waters of modern society: farmland and urban sprawl. Rolling hillsides covered with farms give way to huge developments with their cookie-cutter houses and labyrinthine roadways. Mile after mile, Odie watched as the farmland greenery gave way to the signs of progress and civilization: homes, factories, electrical power towers.

 Every few miles, the presence of hawks hovering, usually in pairs, reminded him of the Lehigh Gorge. Just the sight of their red tails flashing in the sunlight, like a river guide's signaling paddle, was enough to bring him back there.

 He liked it back home, 'on the mountain', but he found he also didn't mind it much 'down here' in the urban areas. He liked some areas more than others, just as there were some women he liked to dance with more than others.

 He thought about what made one woman more enjoyable to dance with than another. He thought that if he could isolate that trait and teach himself how to recognize it he would improve his outings immensely. After several minutes, he concluded, that a lack of expectations and anticipation on her part made for the most enjoyable dances. It didn't matter if she was the best dancer or a beginner, any woman could be the most enjoyable dance partner of the evening, as long as she made no demands on him and followed his lead.

He thought about what made a woman unenjoyable to dance with and his mind raced with the all instances he encountered during unpleasant dances. Walls, he thought, definitely walls, some women had these barriers, invisible barriers that kept him out. He could tell by the connection that she wasn't letting him into her 'space', that there was something she needed to keep from him and it impeded his ability to connect with her...then he realized what he had just said to himself and said out loud, "it IS about connection!"

By six p.m., he was at the Mid-County exit of the turnpike and fully immersed in the ebb and flow of a large metropolitan area that is the suburbs of Philadelphia. Crawling down the Schuylkill Expressway, just after rush hour, its greenery laced with train tunnels, antenna farms and smokestacks, Odie took the Green Lane exit to a quick mart and energized himself with a sixteen-ounce coffee, preparing for a long night of dancing Argentine Tango.

Back on the expressway, he came around a bend and saw the Philadelphia Museum of Art, the place where Sylvester Stallone posed as Rocky Balboa in the famous movie, "Rocky."

In thirty minutes, he was parked outside the dance studio located on the first floor of a four-story building, near the water's edge of the Delaware River on the eastern side of the city, a mile south of the Ben Franklin Bridge.

CHAPTER THIRTEEN

As he entered the studio, he was overwhelmed by an ominous feeling, like a dark cloud passing in front of the sun, he swore he could hear the whirr of helicopter blades, then the cloud passed and he turned inside a foyer to find a woman, seated at a small wooden desk, a small notepad open in front of her. He handed her a ten-dollar bill, told her his name, then proceeded to a long couch where he sat down and began putting on his dance shoes.

By now, Odie could recognize a pattern in how the music for different styles of tango; Argentine Tango, Vals and Milonga; was presented. First, there were three tandas of Argentine Tango, then a tanda of Vals, then three more tandas of Argentine Tango, then a tanda of Milonga. Each song lasted about three minutes or less.

Odie also was becoming quite familiar with the rules of milonga, having broken them so many times. Couples danced in a line-of-dance, moving counter-clockwise around the outer edge of the room in two lanes, much like a highway running in a circle. Each couple danced immediately behind the couple in front of them. Each person in a couple would dance around their partner, as they waited for the couple in front of them to proceed, whereby they could move forward. In this way, the whole roomful of dancers moved in a cohesive, pulsating manner and seemed to have a rhythm all their own.

At times, one couple would inevitably crash into another couple. Often, there were injuries, as a woman flailing around a three-inch spike at the end of her heel is likely to cause. It was incumbent upon the men, in this situation, to apologize politely, each accepting the blame for the collision...in a perfect world things would work this way. Sometimes brief arguments broke out, then the two men would shake hands and continue dancing.

Using the technique called cabaceo, Odie invited women to dance. He was familiar with a few of the regulars in the Philadelphia tango scene and he was finding it difficult not to make eye contact.

Tango was teaching Odie another lesson in life. He found this rewarding. Dancing provided an amazing number of analogies to life, as in, "Life is like a dance". This lesson was on how to function at a social event with many women at the event angry with him.

Some women were mad at him because he was too loud and too coarse in his speech. Others were victims along the learning curve of his highway to dance proficiency. The veteran's latest offenses against members of the female persuasion mostly owed to his social skills as a dancer. Not asking a woman to dance, it seems, was just as offensive as a loud outburst or a stubbed toe, probably even more.

Tonight he danced with disinterest, enjoying the tango music and leading simple patterns, not caring if he was being too boring or repetitive. He made it a point to dance with all new women unless he was cornered by a regular.

After several hours, he noticed a woman of medium height, attired in a black dress angling for his attention. She was not socializing with the other ladies, as some women were inclined to do. She was here to dance. He knew her type and he was having fun casually avoiding her as she moved from couch to chair to another couch, in an attempt to catch his eye without being too conspicuous. She had short brown hair. Her face was plain, devoid of makeup and she wore no jewelry or a watch. He found her simple appearance alluring, much like an evergreen tree at Christmas time before it is decorated.

At the start of a Vals tanda, he made eye contact and looked towards the dance floor. She nodded ever so slightly and moved towards him. They embraced. Inspired by watching Tiresias engage Cassie earlier in the day, he took his time and enjoyed the tender moment of impact. He held out his left hand at the height of her head and she hung her right hand on it like a hat on a rack. Her hand felt small and soft on his.

Moving his right hand around her back to her shoulder blade, he waited to see if she wanted to dance close or open embrace. She moved in, to his surprise, for a deep embrace without leaning on him too heavily, as an inexperienced tanguera might.

Her soft hair pushed gently into his cheek. The music began and he waited to feel the rise and fall of her breathing. When he did, he shifted weight to begin. He could feel the softness of her breast, pressing ever so slightly against his torso, her weight shifting to match his. He paused and she waited.

"The passion in tango," he remembered Jack Stueben telling him, "is not in the movements but in the pauses."

He noticed the pleasant odor of soap. She smelled very fresh. He feigned a movement to the side and she reacted, moving slightly to the side and withdrawing in unison with him.

Odie heard many times, tango is a conversation, and he found the adage to be true. The discussion was conducted entirely through body language without verbal communication. The absence of audible intercourse allowed for a more intimate interaction between two strangers but there were still many rules to be followed.

Although they were entwined deeply within each others' arms, it was incumbent on the man to allow the woman room to maneuver within his grasp. This required him to keep his hand open upon her back, if he closed the ends of his fingers to complete the embrace, she would feel constricted and might end the dance. The woman could end the dance at any time.

It was up to the leader to initiate the movements to a rhythm within the music. The woman would complete the movement, or follow, and wait for her cue to begin the next step. Each individual step in tango is complete, separate, though it may seem fluid to the casual observer. The difficulty of tango is in the communication between the two partners and in establishing a proper connection. They must be able to feel every movement of each other however slight. The better two people are at setting up a physical link the more enjoyment they are able to extract from the music and each other.

He moved to the side, completing the weight change from his right to his left foot, then he paused. He applied a slight upward pressure with his right hand beneath her right shoulder blade, the skin of her back felt soft, the thin strap of her bra lay at the bottom of his finger. She moved with him and, as he paused and lifted, she traced tiny gentle circles on the wooden floor with the toes of her free foot. He did not need to see her shoe in order to tell what she was doing, he could feel the vibration of each circle ride up her leg to her spine and into his embrace...and it felt nice.

Odie was impressed by this woman's ability to follow so completely. She did not move until he moved. He could see her entire demeanor was one of total concentration on his every movement, yet she was in constant motion, her free foot always tracing circles, or dashes, or diagonals, on the floor. If he gave her an extra beat to complete the movement, she would use it to add an embellishment of some sort that he found very pleasing.

The tanda ended signaled by the cortina, the short piece of non-tango music used to separate the different tandas. A man is only obligated to dance one tanda with a woman and the woman can end the dance at any time. When the cortina is played, if either partner says, "thank you very much," the dance is over. If the two wish to continue dancing for another tanda, they simply wait for the cortina to end without leaving the dance floor.

This was the moment he tried to speak about to Cassie at a picnic table in another world, another lifetime it seemed. It was the moment of silence between tandas. He was with a partner with whom he wished to continue dancing. He looked around the room to keep from looking at her directly, perhaps making her uncomfortable. Cortinas last about thirty seconds but there is no set length. After fifteen seconds, he was relieved to see her still standing next to him but he knew she could still leave.

The interlude ended and a tanda of Argentine Tango began. The couple embraced, this time, a little bit closer, with more familiarity and less inhibition. Argentine Tango, Odie realized at this moment, to the point of being a 'full believer', an apostle of the faith, is a very sensual dance.

Sometimes, he surmised, romantically, dancing tango results in the contact between two souls. Like the river, this dance was able to touch his very soul, the most difficult part of a person to reach and the most sensitive.

When he danced tango, he found that sometimes, not all the time, but often enough to repeat in hopes of it happening again, wisps of smoke from the ephemeral fire of his soul would intermingle with wisps of smoke from the ephemeral fire of the soul of his dance partner...then the song would end, the dance would stop and the smoke would dissipate. When he walked away from the woman, he found himself affected deeply by the experience and no longer the same person; she was now a part of him forever.

Soon, the tanda was over and the couple waited through yet another cortina as a tanda of Milonga began.

Milonga is often a much faster-paced version of tango and, at the end of the tanda, the two were completely winded and agreed to end the dance with the customary, "thank you very much." Each went back to seats at opposite sides of the room. He found himself experiencing that rare tango feeling as if he were trailing some of her 'smoke'.

Soon, the gathering ended and Odie left for another milonga that did not start until 11 p.m. It is not unusual for milongueros, the name for people who dance tango, to dance until dawn, with the end often coming when all the couples have decided they can no longer move.

The next place was a parlor, located across town, several blocks west of where he was now. He did not get there until after midnight and partook of the free coffee and appetizers as he watched other couples moving around the floor. He was tired but not ready to go home. Sitting on a sofa in the dimly lit room, the music was so loud he did not hear his phone notifying him of a new message.

Just before 2 a.m., the woman in the black dress appeared again. This time he played no games. They made eye contact right away and began to dance. He found his ability improving after dancing for several hours. He was feeling adventurous in his leads. When he led a colgada, a movement where both partners share the same axis and swing around in a circle, the two executed the move with great precision and he could not help but smile. She smiled, too, not broadly but the small, gentle smile of pure satisfaction.

Odie felt himself beginning to get aroused. He knew he would not be able to suppress it, nor did he want to suppress it. He let it go, feeling confident the bulge in his pants would be hidden in the dim light. He felt young once again. He waited for her to notice and to walk away but she never did. The two danced together for an hour, tanda after tanda, settling into movements that gradually grew slower and slower as their embrace grew more intimate. His erection faded as if it had given up on the siege of a hilltop fortress, too strong to be overpowered. He was in a semi-catatonic state where all he wanted to do was hold this woman and move to the tango music.

When they finally sat down, after 3 a.m., she said, with a heavy British accent, "Would you like to tango by the pier when the sun comes up? I know a nice dock on the river that would be perfect for tango."

He agreed robotically, unable to say much more than, "yes," and not wanting to say anything to ruin his chance to spend more time with this sultry, sensual woman.

Once having his consent, she added, "Oh, would you mind terribly if we stopped by the hospital first? I've got to check in on a patient and it's not quite yet getting light out, would it be a bother?"

He assured her he didn't mind at all and followed her like a lost puppy out of the dance parlor to her car.

CHAPTER FOURTEEN

Big Jane and Jose sat on a patch of grass, next to the old railroad grade converted into a smooth biking trail. Today was a weekday and it was unlikely anyone would come riding past. They were profoundly busy doing nothing as they waited for the ambulance to arrive. The narcotic effect of the hashish turned their thoughts into broken fragments that they imagined floating around until the next idea burst into their addled brains and drifted out into space.

The pain from Jose's broken leg was intense. After a small pipe, filled with a dark brown powder that smelled like tar, was lit and consumed, the pain became bearable.

Jane was not a compassionate woman. Providing comfort to the injured was not one of her best skills. She was good at stabilizing injuries and transporting the wounded. She did not fight the tranquilizing effects of the white smoke coming from the brass pipe where a tiny ember had burned to fine ash. She was not Florence Nightingale, nor was she a cold-hearted stone, so she did what she could to help ease the throbbing pain in Jose's leg, even if it was illegal.

River guides are not saints.

She chewed on the end of a long blade of straw grass, crushing the end completely with her perfect set of white teeth, before reaching down and grabbing another one. A small pile of flattened grass-blades lay on the ground before her.

A red-tailed hawk circled overhead. Jane watched a trio of crows fly out from the forest canopy to harass the raptor and drive it away. The hawk swooped and dived, trying to evade the smaller birds without success. The black avians accomplished their task after several minutes of ariel engagements. The hawk departed to find a meal somewhere else.

A half hour passed before the stillness of the forest was broken by the noise of an all-terrain vehicle. In a few moments, Jane could see a camouflaged, four-wheeled vehicle coming down a path through the tree-covered hillside. She followed the sound of its engine as it wound its way down the hill to the bike path. It entered the biking route a hundred yards south of the two dopeheads.

She could see the helmeted rider, looking up and down the trail, like some sort of futuristic traffic cop riding through the woods to apprehend wilderness lawbreakers. The driver turned the handlebars and slowly advanced towards the injured police officer and the river guide. It covered the distance in a few short moments and they confronted each other.

Jane stood on the side of the trail, adrenalin coursing through her veins, bringing blood to her brain. Now she was fully alert. She stared at the rider, a man dressed in a thick, long-sleeved flannel shirt to protect his arms from swinging branches as he plowed through the woods on his gas-powered mobile couch. He wore thick dungarees and black, high-topped boots. The vehicle had two strap-down racks, one on the front and back; the back held a small cooler. On the front, was a vest with a hunting license visible through a clear plastic window in a leather pouch.

What held Jane's attention, however, was the presence of a small shotgun strapped to the handlebars. She surmised it might be for hunting turkey, however something about the posture of the man on the ATV told her it might be for anything else.

She continued to watch the helmeted rider as he stared back at her, his entire face hidden by a full-feature dust mask and black goggles. He revved the engine, trying to startle the woman standing before him. She stood still, unflinching. Reaching forward, he turned the key off and the engine died.

Now the forest was quiet once more but the peaceful feeling was gone. The presence of the gun changed the dynamic of the woodland setting.

Big Jane had encountered these hillbillies before. Usually they had guns. Usually they were content to put the fear of God into her then leave, satisfied to scare a woman in the woods.

This encounter was not going to be like that.

The man on the ATV was Frankie Hanks, a veteran marine who served two tours in Iraq. Extremely proud of his wartime atrocities of rape and pillage, the young Mr. Hanks boasted often of his exploits, brazenly confessing to crimes against his superior officers.

Frankie was also the brother of a wild girl from the rural areas bordering the Lehigh Gorge State Park. Her name was Tammy Hanks before she married a man named George Tucker and became Tammy Tucker.

One night, Tammy got into a fight with George, her truck-driving husband and left him, suitcases packed, swearing never to return.

She was gone a month when George met Big Jane at the scene of an accident; a van killed a motorcyclist at an intersection in the middle of farm country. She was driving the ambulance. The two talked and began dating.

When Tammy found out, she decided to return and ruin the lives of two innocent adults struggling to make a living on the Pocono Plateau.

Frankie removed his helmet to reveal a head topped with a mat of bright, red curly hair. His eyes were a dull green, set on either side of a large red nose that had been broken many times in bar fights.

He smiled wryly. His green teeth nearly matched his eyes. There was a gap on the top row of teeth. An Arab prostitute he was in the process of raping in a sewer in a Baghdad ghetto, hit him in the face with the leg of a broken chair, knocking out one of his green teeth.

"Janey Heeney," he said, dropping his helmet, dust mask and goggles to the ground. They hit with a hard thud. "What a coincidence, meeting you way out here. I guess I knew I'd run into you sooner or later." He said, running his left hand through his thick hair.

The button on the cuff of his sleeve was open and his forearm was visible. She could see a large scar that ran from his knuckles, on either side of his index finger, all the way down his forearm to his elbow. The scar was thick and dark. It stood out clearly against his pale skin.

Jane's dirty-blond hair blew across her face, dislodged by a strong, cold breeze. The wind blowing upstream was at the head of a cold front, preceding a thunderstorm in the canyon. The clouds in the sky foretold the advancing foul weather.

With an air of defiance, Jane said, "What do you want, Frankie?" She knew what he wanted. She knew it wasn't going to be good for her.

Frankie boasted many times about what he was going to do to the woman who stole his sister's husband. Word got back to her through the gossip grapevine of the barroom scene.

"Who's your friend?" Frankie asked, so matter-of-factly and without a hint of malice.

Jane looked to Jose and back to Frankie. In that short span of time, he unhooked his shotgun and pointed it in her direction. The barrel drooped towards the ground. It wasn't aimed directly at her but it could easily be raised to target her vitals.

The river guide's eyes betrayed the fear growing behind them as they darted left and right. She was looking for a chance to escape and words were not going to get her out of this situation. Her only hope lay in the man with the shotgun being distracted long enough for her to get to the river...she would be safe there, the river would protect her.

Frankie Hanks began a long tirade about his sister. How she was wronged. How the Pendulum of Justice finally swung back in the right direction. He ranted about punishment and how it was as cleansing for the punisher, as it was for the punished.

During this diatribe, Jose attempted to establish a dialog with the raging hillbilly and was rewarded with a shotgun blast to the belly.

There would be no dialog.

The policeman's body rolled violently into the thick underbrush, propelled by the force of the gun blast. There was no movement from the thicket where his body lay, covered by the growing shadows of trees.

The sun was sinking behind the steep canyon walls. The light was getting dim.

Without pausing to catch his breath, or even acknowledge the presence of the other man, the fervid, military-trained mountain man continued his oration until he decided it was now time for the penalty to be delivered.

Big Jane quaked with fear until the shot had been fired. Now she calmed and steeled herself for whatever was about to happen. It was going to be bad but she knew bad. The river punished her enough for her to know what bad can be.

Withdrawing inside herself mentally, she abandoned her body to the pain she was sure this man desired to inflict upon her. Her breathing steadied and her eyes became vacant.

Frankie made her stand against a tree and wrap her arms around it. He bound her wrists with long, plastic ties.

He proceeded to beat her like a dog. He beat her worse than a dog.

From a shallow ditch, concealed by the forest's undergrowth, Jose watched the entire horrid event. It was a miracle he remained conscious and that he managed to hang onto his cell phone to text a friend working as a 9-1-1 dispatcher in New York City. In spite of the point-blank discharge by a 20-gauge shotgun, Jose focused on survival. Such is the tenacity of the NYPD.

He was bleeding to death.

Captain Jack Stueben, CIA, had been monitoring cellular traffic in that area of the Lehigh River Gorge since Odie texted him earlier in the day. He then ordered two Bureau of Homeland Security helicopters to conduct a training mission in the airspace over the Pocono Plateau. When he picked up Jose's message he commanded the chopper crews to take action.

They appeared overhead suddenly, the sound of their approach hidden by the howls of wind coming up the canyon ahead of the thunder and lightning. Their whirring blades exhaled mightily into the woods with thunderous breath. The two Blackhawks beat down whole trees, like a pair of mighty and angry gods.

Frankie Hanks, pummeling Jane Heeney, was too consumed with his lust for violent rage to notice the presence of the military helicopters. He didn't look up until it was too late to escape. A voice boomed over a megaphone, a gunner hung out the side on a swivel chair, pointing the barrel of a machine gun right at him.

A bright spotlight shone down from the sky, bright as the sun.

The policeman felt himself getting weak and knew death was near. He crawled towards the tree.

A figure, clad in a green jumpsuit, descended a long rope from one of the choppers, subdued the assailant and freed the bound woman.

Jose managed to drag himself to a standing position by grabbing onto a tall sapling and hoisting himself up with his arms. He was only a few feet from the handcuffed Mr. Hanks.

Flashing his badge to his rescuer, he pointed to his bleeding abdomen and to the helicopter. As the agent turned to establish visual contact with the helicopter, Jose pulled a gun out from underneath his green spray jacket, touched the tip of it against Frankie Hanks' head and pulled the trigger.

The crew of the military helicopter watched in stunned horror as they saw Frankie Hanks' head disappear like a red water balloon exploding on the head of a pin. They saw Jose collapse flat onto his back, blood oozing all about his midsection.

The captain of the helicopter shouted into his headset, "POI has been neutralized, live capture not possible." Then he barked several commands to the crew and his team sprung into action.

In seconds, a basket descended from the airship and onto the ground. A woman in a green jumpsuit leapt out of the basket and ran to the comatose Big Jane, shined a small flashlight in her eyes, then ran to Jose. The first crewmember on the ground, separated Jose from his gun and held him while the woman cut open his jacket with scissors to examine his wound. She discarded another smaller pistol lodged in his waistband, frisked him quickly for more weapons, then signaled her comrade to assist her in getting the wounded police officer into the basket.

In a minute, Jose disappeared into the sky filled with storm-laden clouds and two helicopters. Another minute passed and the basket came back down to pick up the female kayak guide.

In the span of six minutes, Jose, Big Jane and the dead body of Frankie Hanks were all loaded onboard the air transport, whisked into the heavens and heading south.

Another minute later and the forest was still except for the rustle of leaves blown by the wind.

CHAPTER FIFTEEN

Speeding through the avenues of downtown Philadelphia in his green van, Odie followed the woman in the black dress driving a yellow BMW from the milonga to a hospital near the Schuylkill River. Donning a white jacket as she exited her vehicle, she moved quickly through automated doorways and into an elevator. Like a mouse in a well-known maze, Odie right behind her, she navigated the labyrinthine passageways of the hospital like a heat-seeking missile, aided by her security card and doctor's identification badge.

Forty floors up and half a block inside the gargantuan structure of steel, concrete and electronic devices, she came to a stop outside a hospital room. She grabbed a flip chart hanging from a hook at eye level next to the doorframe.

" I'll just be a moment," the British woman said, "she came in last night, all beat up but not really damaged too badly. Insurance company won't pay for her to stay for two days, so I've got to make sure she's good to go. Cheerio." With that said, she disappeared inside the room.

Odie sat on a small sofa and stared at a gurney along the wall next to the doorway. It held, what Odie knew from his three deployments and events earlier in the day, a body bag, all zipped up. He could tell the bag was in use. Something inside him told him to look away from the stretcher but he would not. He was afraid that if he looked away a dead man might appear to him. He forced himself to keep looking at the body bag, not closing his eyes, fearing even to blink.

A nurse appeared out of a corridor and walked past, they exchanged greetings. Looking back to the gurney, he saw Jose sitting on the edge, swinging his legs playfully, still wearing his wetsuit bottoms and bright green spray jacket.

The hairs on Odie's arms and on the back of his neck bristled and vibrated. He could feel adrenalin rushing through his veins and felt the urge to flee but he could not move.

"You look like you seen a fucking ghost!" Jose said.

Odie didn't answer. He couldn't speak, he just sat there, slack-jawed.

"Y'know, I learned my lesson," the spirit continued, "Life humbled me but I took it and now I get to move on. But you gotta fucking know, she needs you. I have to tell you this before I can go. She's okay, but you have to take her back to the River, she'll be okay there."

Odie, dazed and confused, managed to utter, "What?"

Jose nodded his head towards the room where the doctor was.

Odie looked towards the doorway and back to the ghost of the dead policeman but it was gone. The body bag was, as it had been, zipped and still.

His face was now ashen white. He sensed the events that transpired after he left the river. Somehow the New York cop died and ended up here. Someone he knew was in the room the doctor was now exiting.

In an almost cryptic voice, Odie asked, his hands trembling, "Is the woman in there named Jane Heeney?"

The doctor looked at her notepad, her facial expression changing from a smile to one of confusion, and said, "Yes, yes it is, but how did you know?"

"She's my ex." he replied, "I don't know how I know, but I've got to take her home."

"Why, certainly," the doctor said, disappointed, but aware something strange and mystical had happened. "There's a process...but I'll get an orderly and we'll start right away. I'm so sorry, not just about the dance. It's someone you know. It always hurts. She made them give her a full blood transfusion, in case of HIV infection, she should be all right...but there's the mental part of it. I'm sorry."

Forty-five minutes later, as the sun began to rise on the eastern horizon, above the New Jersey Pine Barrens, Odie Larson drove his green van across the Ben Franklin Bridge; Big Jane Heeney sat in the passengers seat, dressed in a brown fleece sweater and black fleece pants, his after-river clothes on cold days. He took the long way home, crossing over to New Jersey on the Ben Franklin Bridge and coming back to Pennsylvania on the Betsy Ross Bridge, a few miles upstream on the Delaware River.

She needed him to cross it twice so she could see the river flowing to the sea and take comfort in the swirling eddies of the moving water.

She sat silently, clasping a half-empty bottle of ice-cold beer Odie had saved for his ride home from tango. She was on her third beer by the time they came across the Betsy Ross Bridge. As they drove across the span, both staring at the river, two

Blackhawk helicopters zoomed above them, heading north.

The war found them both, Odie thought, as he turned off the exit ramp of the bridge and onto the interstate. The Delaware River glistened in the early morning sunshine, reflecting images of brilliant foils of gold. He reached into the white cooler, grabbed himself a beer and headed home.

Jack Stueben lay in his bed staring at a crack in the ceiling. The strong smell of fresh tea, cinnamon and cloves filled the room. Bunny appeared, scantily clad and bearing a tray of tea cups and snacks, smiling softly.

"When are you going to let that man know your 'accident' was all a ruse, Jack?" Bunny asked.

Jack replied, pensively, bending his right leg beneath the covers, "Probably never, Bunny," he said, pausing to take a deep breath before continuing, "with the death of Frankie Hanks I'm back at ground zero. It's like all the clues have been washed away in this case. I hate to use Odie like that but I think he's going to be alright. Believe me, he's a lot safer not knowing. He's humble and I got a good feeling he'll be able to navigate his way through no matter what we send his way."

The End

Made in the USA
Charleston, SC
23 October 2011